Uncle Remus

Uncle Remus

TRADE MARK, REG. U. S. PAT. OFFICE

HIS SONGS AND HIS SAYINGS

By JOEL CHANDLER HARRIS

New and Revised Edition

WITH OVER 100 ILLUSTRATIONS BY

A. B. FROST

GROSSET & DUNLAP   *Publishers*   NEW YORK

Printed in the United States of America

PREFACE AND DEDICATION
TO THE NEW EDITION

To Arthur Burdette Frost:

MY DEAR FROST: I am expected to supply a preface for this new edition of my first book—to advance from behind the curtain, as it were, and make a fresh bow to the public that has dealt with Uncle Remus in so gentle and generous a fashion. For this event the lights are to be rekindled, and I am expected to respond in some formal way to an encore that marks the fifteenth anniversary of the book. There have been other editions—how many I do not remember —but this is to be an entirely new one, except as to the matter: new type, new pictures, and new binding.

But, as frequently happens on such occasions, I am at a loss for a word. I seem to see before me the smiling faces of thousands of children—some young and fresh, and some wearing the friendly marks of age, but all children at heart—and not an unfriendly face among them. And out of the confusion, and while I am trying hard to speak the right word, I seem to hear a voice lifted above the rest, saying: "You have made some of us happy." And so I feel my heart fluttering and my lips trembling, and I have to bow silently and turn away, and hurry back into the obscurity that fits me best.

Phantoms! Children of dreams! True, my dear Frost; but if you could see the thousands of letters that have come to me from far and near, and all fresh from the hearts and hands of children, and from men and women who have not forgotten how to be children, you would not wonder at the dream. And such a dream can do no harm. Insubstantial though it may be, I would not at this hour exchange it for all the fame won by my mightier brethren of the pen—whom I most humbly salute.

Measured by the material developments that have compressed years of experience into the space of a day, thus increasing the possibilities of life, if not its beauty, fifteen years constitute the old age of a book. Such a survival might almost be said to be due to a tiny sluice of green sap under the gray bark. Where it lies in the matter of this book, or what its source—if, indeed, it be really there—is more of a mystery to my middle age than it was to my prime.

But it would be no mystery at all if this new edition were to be more popular than the old one. Do you know why? Because you have taken it under your hand and made it yours. Because you have breathed the breath of life into these amiable brethren of wood and field. Because, by a stroke here and a touch there, you have conveyed into their quaint antics the illumination of your own inimitable humor, which is as true to our sun and soil as it is to the spirit and essence of the matter set forth.

The book was mine, but now you have made it yours, both sap and pith. Take it, therefore, my dear Frost, and believe me, faithfully yours,

JOEL CHANDLER HARRIS.

vi

INTRODUCTION

I AM advised by my publishers that this book is to be included in their catalogue of humorous publications, and this friendly warning gives me an opportunity to say that however humorous it may be in effect, its intention is perfectly serious; and, even if it were otherwise, it seems to me that a volume written wholly in dialect must have its solemn, not to say melancholy, features. With respect to the Folk-Lore series, my purpose has been to preserve the legends themselves in their original simplicity, and to wed them permanently to the quaint dialect—if, indeed, it can be called a dialect—through the medium of which they have become a part of the domestic history of every Southern family; and I have endeavored to give to the whole a genuine flavor of the old plantation.

Each legend has its variants, but in every instance I have retained that particular version which seemed to me to be the most characteristic, and have given it without embellishment and without exaggeration.

The dialect, it will be observed, is wholly different
from that of the Hon. Pompey Smash and his literary
descendants, and different also from the intolerable
misrepresentations of the minstrel stage, but it is at
least phonetically genuine. Nevertheless, if the lan-
guage of Uncle Remus fails to give vivid hints of the
really poetic imagination of the Negro; if it fails to
embody the quaint and homely humor which was his
most prominent characteristic; if it does not suggest a
certain picturesque sensitiveness—a curious exaltation
of mind and temperament not to be defined by words
—then I have reproduced the form of the dialect
merely, and not the essence, and my attempt may be
accounted a failure. At any rate, I trust I have been
successful in presenting what must be, at least to a
large portion of American readers, a new and by no
means unattractive phase of Negro character—a phase
which may be considered a curiously sympathetic
supplement to Mrs. Stowe's wonderful defense of
slavery as it existed in the South. Mrs. Stowe, let me
hasten to say, attacked the possibilities of slavery
with all the eloquence of genius; but the same genius
painted the portrait of the Southern slave-owner, and
defended him.

A number of the plantation legends originally appeared in the columns of a daily newspaper—*The Atlanta Constitution*—and in that shape they attracted
the attention of various gentlemen who were kind

enough to suggest that they would prove to be valuable contributions to myth-literature. It is but fair to
say that ethnological considerations formed no part
of the undertaking which has resulted in the publication of this volume. Professor J. W. Powell, of the
Smithsonian Institution, who is engaged in an investigation of the mythology of the North American Indians, informs me that some of Uncle Remus's stories
appear in a number of different languages, and in
various modified forms, among the Indians; and he is
of the opinion that they are borrowed by the Negroes
from the red-men. But this, to say the least, is ex-
tremely doubtful, since another investigator (Mr.
Herbert H. Smith, author of Brazil and the Amazons)
has met with some of these stories among tribes of
South American Indians, and one in particular he
has traced to India, and as far east as Siam. Mr. Smith
has been kind enough to send me the proof-sheets of
his chapter on The Myths and Folk-Lore of the
Amazonian Indians, in which he reproduces some of
the stories which he gathered while exploring the
Amazons.

In the first of his series, a tortoise falls from a tree
upon the head of a jaguar and kills him; in one of
Uncle Remus's stories, the terrapin falls from a shelf
in Miss Meadows's house and stuns the fox, so that the
latter fails to catch the rabbit. In the next, a jaguar
catches a tortoise by the hind-leg as he is disappear-

ing in his hole; but the tortoise convinces him he is holding a root, and so escapes; Uncle Remus tells how the fox endeavored to drown the terrapin, but turned him loose because the terrapin declared his tail to be only a stump-root. Mr. Smith also gives the story of how the tortoise outran the deer, which is identical as to incident with Uncle Remus's story of how Brer Tarrypin outran Brer Rabbit. Then there is the story of how the tortoise pretended that he was stronger than the tapir. He tells the latter he can drag him into the sea, but the tapir retorts that he will pull the tortoise into the forest and kill him besides. The tortoise thereupon gets a vine-stem, ties one end around the body of the tapir, and goes to the sea, where he ties the other end to the tail of a whale. He then goes into the wood, midway between them both, and gives the vine a shake as a signal for the pulling to begin. The struggle between the whale and tapir goes on until each thinks the tortoise is the strongest of animals. Compare this with the story of the terrapin's contest with the bear, in which Miss Meadows's bed-cord is used instead of a vine-stem. One of the most characteristic of Uncle Remus's stories is that in which the rabbit proves to Miss Meadows and the girls that the fox is his riding-horse. This is almost identical with a story quoted by Mr. Smith, where the jaguar is about to marry the deer's daughter. The cotia—a species of rodent—is also in love with her, and he tells the deer that he can make a riding-horse of the jaguar. "Well," says the deer, "if you can make the jaguar carry you, you shall have my daughter." Thereupon the story proceeds pretty much as Uncle Remus tells it of the fox and rabbit. The cotia finally jumps from the jaguar and takes refuge in a hole, where an owl is set to watch him, but he flings sand in the owl's eyes and escapes. In another story given by Mr. Smith, the cotia is very thirsty, and, seeing a man coming with a jar on his head, lies down in the road in front of him, and repeats this until the man puts down his jar to go back after all the dead cotias he has seen. This is almost identical with Uncle Remus's story of how the rabbit robbed the fox of his game. In a story from Upper Egypt, a fox lies down in the road in front of a man who is carrying fowls to market, and finally succeeds in securing them.

This similarity extends to almost every story quoted by Mr. Smith, and some are so nearly identical as to point unmistakably to a common origin; but when and where? When did the Negro or the North American Indian ever come in contact with the tribes of South America? Upon this point the author of Brazil and the Amazons, who is engaged in making a critical and comparative study of these myth-stories, writes:

"I am not prepared to form a theory about these stories. There can be no doubt that some of them, found among the Negroes and the Indians, had a common origin. The most natural solution would be to suppose that they originated in Africa, and were carried to South America by the Negro slaves. They are certainly found among the Red Negroes; but, unfortunately for the African theory, it is equally certain that they are told by savage Indians of the Amazons Valley, away up on the Tapajos, Red Negro, and Tapurá. These Indians hardly ever see a Negro, and their languages are very distinct from the broken Portuguese spoken by the slaves. The form of the stories, as recounted in the Tupi and Mundurucú languages, seems to show that they were originally formed in those languages or have long been adopted in them.

"It is interesting to find a story from Upper Egypt (that of the fox who pretended to be dead) identical with an Amazonian story, and strongly resembling one found by you among the Negroes. Varnhagen, the Brazilian historian (now Visconde de Rio Branco), tried to prove a relationship between the ancient Egyptians, or other Turanian stock, and the Tupi Indians. His theory rested on rather a slender basis, yet it must be confessed that he had one or two strong points. Do the resemblances between Old and New World stories point to a similar conclusion? It would be hard to say with the material that we now have.

"One thing is certain. The animal stories told by the Negroes in our Southern States and in Brazil were brought by them from Africa. Whether they originated there, or with the Arabs, or Egyptians, or with yet more ancient nations, must still be an open question. Whether the Indians got them from the Negroes or from some earlier source is equally uncertain. We have seen enough to know that a very interesting line of investigation has been opened."

Professor Hartt, in his Amazonian Tortoise Myths, quotes a story from the Riverside Magazine of November, 1868, which will be recognized as a variant of one given by Uncle Remus. I venture to append it here, with some necessary verbal and phonetic alterations, in order to give the reader an idea of the difference between the dialect of the cotton plantations, as used by Uncle Remus, and the lingo in vogue on the rice plantations and Sea Islands of the South Atlantic States:

"One time B'er Deer an' B'er Cooter (Terrapin) was courtin', and de lady did bin lub B'er Deer mo' so dan B'er Cooter. She did bin lub B'er Cooter, but she lub B'er Deer de morest. So de noung lady say to B'er Deer and B'er Cooter bofe dat dey mus' hab a ten-mile race, an' de one dat beats, she will go marry him.

"So B'er Cooter say to B'er Deer: 'You has got mo' longer legs dan I has, but I will run you. You run ten mile on land, and I will run ten mile on de water!'

"So B'er Cooter went an' git nine er his fam'ly, an' put one at ebery mile-pos', and he hisse'f, what was to run wid B'er Deer, he was right in front of de young lady's do', in de broom-grass.

"Dat mornin' at nine o'clock, B'er Deer he did met B'er Cooter at de fus mile-pos', wey dey was to start fum. So he call: 'Well, B'er Cooter, is you ready? Go long!' As he git on to de nex' mile-pos', he say: 'B'er Cooter!' B'er

Cooter say: 'Hullo!' B'er Deer say: 'You dere?' B'er
Cooter say: 'Yes, B'er Deer, I dere too.'

"Nex' mile-pos' he jump, B'er Deer say: 'Hullo, B'er
Cooter!' B'er Cooter say: 'Hullo, B'er Deer! you dere
too?' B'er Deer say: 'Ki! it look like you gwine fer tie
me; it look like we gwine fer de gal tie!'

"W'en he git to de nine-mile pos' he tought he git dere
fus, 'cause he mek two jump; so he holler: 'B'er Cooter!'
B'er Cooter answer: 'You dere too?' B'er Deer say: 'It
look like you gwine tie me.' B'er Cooter say: 'Go long,
B'er Deer. I git dere in due season time,' which he does,
and wins de race."

The story of the Rabbit and the Fox, as told by the
Southern negroes, is artistically dramatic in this: it
progresses in an orderly way from a beginning to a
well-defined conclusion, and is full of striking epi-
sodes that suggest the culmination. It seems to me to
be to a certain extent allegorical, albeit such an in-
terpretation may be unreasonable. At least it is a
fable thoroughly characteristic of the Negro; and it
needs no scientific investigation to show why he
selects as his hero the weakest and most harmless of
all animals, and brings him out victorious in contests
with the bear, the wolf, and the fox. It is not virtue
that triumphs, but helplessness; it is not malice, but
mischievousness. It would be presumptious in me to
offer an opinion as to the origin of these curious
myth-stories; but, if ethnologists should discover that
they did not originate with the African, the proof to

that effect should be accompanied with a good deal of persuasive eloquence.

Curiously enough, I have found few Negroes who will acknowledge to a stranger that they know anything of these legends; and yet to relate one of the stories is the surest road to their confidence and esteem. In this way, and in this way only, I have been enabled to collect and verify the folk-lore included in this volume. There is an anecdote about the Irishman and the rabbit which a number of Negroes have told to me with great unction, and which is both funny and characteristic, though I will not undertake to say that it has its origin with the blacks. One day an Irishman who had heard people talking about "mares' nests" was going along the big road—it is always the big road in contradistinction to neighborhood paths and by-paths, called in the vernacular "nigh-cuts"—when he came to a pumpkin-patch. The Irishman had never seen any of this fruit before, and he at once concluded that he had discovered a veritable mare's nest. Making the most of his opportunity, he gathered one of the pumpkins in his arms and went on his way. A pumpkin is an exceedingly awkward thing to carry, and the Irishman had not gone far before he made a misstep, and stumbled. The pumpkin fell to the ground, rolled down the hill into a "brush-heap," and, striking against a stump, was broken. The story continues in the dialect: "W'en de punkin roll in de bresh-heap, out jump a rabbit; en soon's de I'shmuns see dat, he take atter de rabbit en holler: 'Kworp, colty! kworp, colty!' but de rabbit, he des flew." The point of this is obvious.

As to the songs, the reader is warned that it will be found difficult to make them conform to the ordinary rules of versification, nor is it intended that they should so conform. They are written, and are intended to be read, solely with reference to the regular and invariable recurrence of the cæsura, as, for instance, the first stanza of the Revival Hymn:

"Oh, whar | shill we go | w'en de great | day comes |
  Wid de blow | in' er de trumpits | en de bang | in' er de
    drums |
  How man | y po' sin | ners'll be kotch'd | out late
  En fine | no latch | ter de gold | en gate | "

In other words, the songs depend for their melody and rhythm upon the musical quality of *time*, and not upon long or short, accented or unaccented syllables. I am persuaded that this fact led Mr. Sidney Lanier, who is thoroughly familiar with the metrical peculiarities of negro songs, into the exhaustive investigation which has resulted in the publication of his scholarly treatise on The Science of English Verse.

The difference between the dialect of the legends and that of the character-sketches, slight as it is, marks the modifications which the speech of the

Negro has undergone even where education has played no part in reforming it. Indeed, save in the remote country districts, the dialect of the legends has nearly disappeared. I am perfectly well aware that the character-sketches are without permanent interest, but they are embodied here for the purpose of presenting a phase of Negro character wholly distinct from that which I have endeavored to preserve in the legends. Only in this shape, and with all the local allusions, would it be possible to adequately represent the shrewd observations, the curious retorts, the homely thrusts, the quaint comments, and the humorous philosophy of the race of which Uncle Remus is the type.

If the reader not familiar with plantation life will imagine that the myth-stories of Uncle Remus are told night after night to a little boy by an old Negro who appears to be venerable enough to have lived during the period which he describes—who has nothing but pleasant memories of the discipline of slavery—and who has all the prejudices of caste and pride of family that were the natural results of the system; if the reader can imagine all this, he will find little difficulty in appreciating and sympathizing with the air of affectionate superiority which Uncle Remus assumes as he proceeds to unfold the mysteries of plantation lore to a little child who is the product of that practical reconstruction which has been going on to some extent since the war in spite of the politicians. Uncle Remus describes that reconstruction in his Story of the War, and I may as well add here for the benefit of the curious that that story is almost literally true.

J. C. H.

CONTENTS

CONTENTS

UNCLE REMUS INITIATES THE LITTLE BOY

ONE eve-
ning recently,
the lady whom
Uncle Remus
calls "Miss
Sally" missed
her little sev-
en - year - old
boy. Making
search for
him through the house and
through the yard, she heard
the sound of voices in the
old man's cabin, and, looking through the window,
saw the child sitting by
Uncle Remus. His head
rested against the old man's
arm, and he was gazing with an expression of the
most intense interest into the rough, weather-beaten

face, that beamed so kindly upon him. This is what
"Miss Sally" heard:

"Bimeby, one day, arter Brer Fox bin doin' all dat
he could fer ter ketch Brer Rabbit, en Brer Rabbit
bin doin' all he could fer to keep 'im fum it, Brer Fox
say to hisse'f dat he'd put up a game on Brer Rabbit,
en he ain't mo'n got de wuds out'n his mouf twel Brer
Rabbit come a lopin' up de big road, lookin' des ez
plump, en ez fat, en ez sassy ez a Moggin hoss in a
barley-patch.

" 'Hol' on dar, Brer Rabbit,' sez Brer Fox, sezee.

" 'I ain't got time, Brer Fox,' sez Brer Rabbit, sezee,
sorter mendin' his licks.

" 'I wanter have some confab wid you, Brer Rabbit,' sez Brer Fox, sezee.

" 'All right, Brer Fox, but you better holler fum
whar you stan'. I'm monstus full er fleas dis mawnin','
sez Brer Rabbit, sezee.

" 'I seed Brer B'ar yistiddy,' sez Brer Fox, sezee,
'en he sorter rake me over de coals kaze you en me
ain't make frens en live naberly, en I told 'im dat I'd
see you.'

"Den Brer Rabbit scratch one year wid his off
hinefoot sorter jub'usly, en den he ups en sez, sezee:

" 'All a settin', Brer Fox. Spose'n you drap roun'
ter-morrer en take dinner wid me. We ain't got no
great doin's at our house, but I speck de old 'oman en

de chilluns kin sorter scramble roun' en git up sump'n
fer ter stay yo' stummuck.'

"'I'm 'gree'ble, Brer Rabbit,' sez Brer Fox, sezee.

"'Den I'll 'pen' on you,' sez Brer Rabbit, sezee.

"Nex' day, Mr. Rabbit an' Miss Rabbit got up soon,
'fo' day, en raided on a gyarden like Miss Sally's out
dar, en got some cabbiges en some roas'n years, en
some sparrer-grass, en dey fix up a smashin' dinner.
Bimeby one er de little Rabbits, playin' out in de
backyard, come runnin' in hollerin', 'Oh, ma! oh, ma!
I seed Mr. Fox a comin'!' En den Brer Rabbit he
tuck de chilluns by der years en make um set down,
en den him and Miss Rabbit sorter dally roun' waitin'
for Brer Fox. En dey keep on waitin', but no Brer Fox
ain't come. Atter 'while Brer Rabbit goes to de do',
easy like, en peep out, en dar, stickin' fum behime
de cornder, wuz de tip-een'er Brer Fox tail. Den Brer
Rabbit shot de do' en sot down, en put his paws
behime his years en begin fer ter sing:

"'De place wharbouts you spill de grease,
    Right dar youer boun' ter slide,
  An' whar you fine a bunch er ha'r,
    You'll sholy fine de hide.'

"Nex' day, Brer Fox sont word by Mr. Mink, en
skuze hisse'f kaze he wuz too sick fer ter come, en
he ax Brer Rabbit fer to come en take dinner wid
him, en Brer Rabbit say he wuz 'gree'ble.

"Bimeby, w'en de shadders wuz at der shortes',

Brer Rabbit he sorter brush up en santer down ter Brer Fox's house, en w'en he got dar, he hear some-body groanin', en he look in de do' en dar he see Brer Fox settin' up in a rockin' cheer all wrop up wid flannil, en he look mighty weak. Brer Rabbit look all 'roun', he did, but he ain't see no dinner. De dish-pan wuz settin' on de table, en close by wuz a kyarv-in' knife.

" 'Look like you gwineter have chicken fer dinner, Brer Fox,' sez Brer Rabbit, sezee.

" 'Yes, Brer Rabbit, deyer nice, en fresh, en tender,' sez Brer Fox, sezee.

"Den Brer Rabbit sorter pull his mustarsh, en say: 'You ain't got no calamus root, is you, Brer Fox? I done got so now dat I can't eat no chicken 'ceppin

she's seasoned up wid calamus root.' En wid dat Brer
Rabbit lipt out er de do' and dodge 'mong de bushes,
en sot dar watchin' fer Brer Fox; en he ain't watch
long, nudder, kaze Brer Fox flung off de flannil en
crope out er de house en got whar he could cloze in
on Brer Rabbit, en bimeby Brer Rabbit holler out:
'Oh, Brer Fox! I'll des put yo' calamus root out yer
on dish yer stump. Better come git it while hit's
fresh,' and wid dat Brer Rabbit gallop off home. En
Brer Fox ain't never kotch 'im yit, en w'at's mo',
honey, he ain't gwineter."

II

THE WONDERFUL TAR-BABY STORY

"Didn't the fox *never* catch the rabbit, Uncle
Remus?" asked the little boy the next evening.

"He come mighty nigh it, honey, sho's you born—
Brer Fox did. One day atter Brer Rabbit fool 'im wid
dat calamus root, Brer Fox went ter wuk en got 'im
some tar, en mix it wid some turkentime, en fix up a
contrapshun wat he call a Tar-Baby, en he tuck dish
yer Tar-Baby en he sot 'er in de big road, en den he
lay off in de bushes fer to see what de news wuz
gwineter be. En he didn't hatter wait long, nudder,
kaze bimeby here come Brer Rabbit pacin' down de
road—lippity-clippity, clippity-lippity—dez ez sassy
ez a jay-bird. Brer Fox, he lay low. Brer Rabbit come

prancin' 'long twel he spy de Tar-Baby, en den he
fotch up on his behime legs like he wus 'stonished. De
Tar-Baby, she sot dar, she did, en Brer Fox, he lay
low.

" 'Mawnin'!' sez Brer Rabbit, sezee—'nice wedder
dis mawnin',' sezee.

"Tar-Baby ain't sayin' nothin', en Brer Fox, he lay
low.

" 'How duz yo' sym'tums seem ter segashuate?' sez
Brer Rabbit, sezee.

"Brer Fox, he wink his eye slow, en lay low, en de
Tar-Baby, she ain't sayin' nothin'.

" 'How you come on, den? Is you deaf?' sez Brer
Rabbit, sezee. 'Kaze if you is, I kin holler louder,'
sezee.

"Tar-Baby stay
still, en Brer Fox,
he lay low.

" 'Youer stuck
up, dat's w'at you
is,' says Brer Rab-
bit, sezee, 'en I'm
gwineter kyore
you, dat's w'at I'm
a gwineter do,'
sezee.

"Brer Fox, he
sorter chuckle in
his stummick, he

did, but Tar-Baby ain't sayin' nothin'.

" 'I'm gwineter larn you howter talk ter 'spect-
tubble fokes ef hit's de las' ack,' sez Brer Rabbit,
sezee. 'Ef you don't take off dat hat en tell me howdy,
I'm gwineter bus' you wide open,' sezee.

"Tar-Baby stay still, en Brer Fox, he lay low.

"Brer Rabbit keep on axin' 'im, en de Tar-Baby,
she keep on sayin' nothin', twel present'y Brer Rabbit draw back wid his fis', he did, en blip he tuck 'er
side er de head. Right dar's whar he broke his mer-
lasses jug. His fis' stuck, en he can't pull loose. De tar

hilt 'im. But Tar-Baby, she stay still, en Brer Fox, he lay low.

"'Ef you don't lemme loose, I'll knock you agin,' sez Brer Rabbit, sezee, en wid dat he fotch 'er a wipe wid de udder han', en dat stuck. Tar-Baby, she ain't sayin' nothin', en Brer Fox, he lay low.

"'Tu'n me loose, fo' I kick de natal stuffin' outen you,' sez Brer Rabbit, sezee, but de Tar-Baby, she ain't sayin' nothin'. She des hilt on, en den Brer Rabbit lose de use er his feet in de same way. Brer Fox, he lay low. Den Brer Rabbit squall out dat ef de Tar-Baby don't tu'n 'im loose he butt 'er cranksided. En den he butted, en his head got stuck. Den Brer Fox,

he sa'ntered fort', lookin' des ez innercent ez one er
yo' mammy's mockin'-birds.

"'Howdy, Brer Rabbit,' sez Brer Fox, sezee. 'You
look sorter stuck up dis mawnin',' sezee, en den he
rolled on de groun', en laughed en laughed twel he
couldn't laugh no mo'. 'I speck you'll take dinner
wid me dis time, Brer Rabbit. I done laid in some
calamus root, en I ain't gwineter take no skuse,' sez
Brer Fox, sezee."

Here Uncle Remus paused, and drew a two-pound
yam out of the ashes.

"Did the fox eat the rabbit?" asked the little boy
to whom the story had been told.

"Dat's all de fur de tale goes," replied the old man.
"He mout, en den again he moutent. Some say Jedge
B'ar come long en loosed 'im—some say he didn't. I
hear Miss Sally callin'. You better run 'long."

III

WHY MR. POSSUM LOVES PEACE

"One night," said Uncle Remus—taking Miss Sally's
little boy on his knee, and stroking the child's hair
thoughtfully and caressingly—"one night Brer Possum
call by fer Brer Coon, 'cordin' ter greement, en atter
gobblin' up a dish er fried greens en smokin' a seegyar, dey rambled fort' fer ter see how de ballance er
de settlement wuz gittin' 'long. Brer Coon, he wuz

one er deze yer natchul pacers, en he racked 'long
same ez Mars John's bay pony, en Brer Possum he
went in a han'-gallup; en dey got over heap er groun',
mon. Brer Possum, he got his belly full er 'simmons,
en Brer Coon, he scoop up a 'bunnunce er frogs en
tadpoles. Dey amble 'long, dey did, des ez sociable
ez a basket er kittens, twel bimeby dey hear Mr. Dog
talkin' ter hisse'f way off in de woods.

" 'Spozen he runs up on us, Brer Possum, w'at you
gwineter do?' sez Brer Coon, sezee. Brer Possum
sorter laugh 'round de cornders un his mouf.

" 'Oh, ef he come, Brer Coon, I'm gwineter stan'
by you,' sez Brer Possum. 'W'at you gwineter do?'
sezee.

" 'Who? me?' sez Brer Coon. 'Ef he run up onter
me, I lay I give 'im one twis',' sezee."

"Did the dog come?" asked the little boy.

"Go 'way, honey!" responded the old man, in an
impressive tone. "Go way! Mr. Dog, he come en he
come a zoonin'. En he ain't wait fer ter say howdy,
nudder. He des sail inter de two un um. De ve'y fus
pas he make Brer Possum fetch a grin fum year ter
year, en keel over like he wuz dead. Den Mr. Dog, he
sail inter Brer Coon, en right dar's whar he drap his
money purse, kaze Brer Coon wuz cut out fer dat
kinder bizness, en he fa'rly wipe up de face er de yeth
wid 'im. You better b'leeve dat w'en Mr. Dog got a
chance to make hisse'f skase he tuck it, en w'at der

wuz lef' un him went skaddlin' thoo de woods like hit
wuz shot outen a muskit. En Brer Coon, he sorter

lick his cloze inter shape en rack off, en Brer Possum,
he lay dar like he wuz dead, twel bimeby he raise up
sorter keerful like, en w'en he fine de coas' cle'r he
scramble up en scamper off like sumpin was atter
'im.''

Here Uncle Remus paused long enough to pick up
a live coal of fire in his fingers, transfer it to the palm

of his hand, and thence to his clay pipe, which he had been filling—a proceeding that was viewed by the little boy with undisguised admiration. The old man then proceeded:

"Nex' time Brer Possum met Brer Coon, Brer Coon 'fuse ter 'spon' ter his howdy, en dis make Brer Possum feel mighty bad, seein' ez how dey useter make so many 'scurshuns tergedder.

" 'W'at make you hol' yo' head so high, Brer Coon?' sez Brer Possum, sezee.

" 'I ain't runnin' wid cowerds deze days,' sez Brer Coon. 'W'en I wants you I'll sen' fer you,' sezee.

"Den Brer Possum git mighty mad.

" 'Who's enny cowerd?' sezee.

" 'You is,' sez Brer Coon, 'dat's who. I ain't so-shatin' wid dem w'at lays down on de groun' en plays dead w'en dar's a free fight gwine on,' sezee.

"Den Brer Possum grin en laugh fit to kill hisse'f.

" 'Lor', Brer Coon, you don't speck I done dat kaze I wuz 'feared, duz you?' sezee. 'W'y I want no mo' 'feared dan you is dis minnit. W'at wuz dey fer ter be skeered un?' sezee. 'I know'd you'd git away wid Mr. Dog ef I didn't, en I des lay dar watchin' you shake him, waitin' fer ter put in w'en de time come,' sezee.

"Brer Coon tu'n up his nose.

" 'Dat's a mighty likely tale,' sezee, 'w'en Mr. Dog

ain't mo'n tech you 'fo' you keel over, en lay dar stiff,'
sezee. .

" 'Dat's des w'at I wuz gwineter tell you 'bout,' sez
Brer Possum, sezee. 'I want no mo' skeer'd dan you
is right now, en' I wuz fixin' fer ter give Mr. Dog a
sample er my jaw,' sezee, 'but I'm de most ticklish
chap w'at you ever laid eyes on, en no sooner did Mr.
Dog put his nose down yer 'mong my ribs dan I got
ter laughin', en I laughed twel I ain't had no use er
my lim's,' sezee, 'en it's a mussy unto Mr. Dog dat I
wuz ticklish, kaze a little mo' en I'd e't 'im up,' sezee.
'I don't mine fightin', Brer Coon, no mo' dan you duz,'
sezee, 'but I declar' ter grashus ef I kin stan' ticklin'.
Git me in a row whar dey ain't no ticklin' 'lowed, en
I'm your man,' sezee.

"En down ter dis day"—continued Uncle Remus,
watching the smoke from his pipe curl upward over
the little boy's head—"down ter dis day, Brer Possum's bound ter s'render w'en you tech him in de
short ribs, en he'll laugh ef he knows he's gwineter be
smashed fer it."

IV

HOW MR. RABBIT WAS TOO SHARP FOR MR. FOX

"UNCLE REMUS," said the little boy one evening,
when he had found the old man with little or nothing
to do, "did the fox kill and eat the rabbit when he
caught him with the Tar-Baby?"

"Law, honey, ain't I tell you 'bout dat?" replied
the old darkey, chuckling slyly. "I 'clar ter grashus
I ought er tole you dat, but old man Nod wuz ridin'
on my eyeleds 'twel a leetle mo'n I'd a dis'member'd
my own name, en den on to dat here come yo'
mammy hollerin' atter you.

"W'at I tell you w'en I fus' begin? I tole you Brer
Rabbit wuz a monstus soon creetur; leas'ways dat's
w'at I laid out fer ter tell you. Well, den, honey, don't
you go en make no udder calkalashuns, kaze in dem
days Brer Rabbit en his fambly wuz at de head er
de gang w'en enny racket wuz on han', en dar dey
stayed. 'Fo' you begins fer ter wipe yo' eyes 'bout
Brer Rabbit, you wait en see whar'bouts Brer Rabbit

gwineter fetch up at. But dat's needer yer ner dar.

"W'en Brer Fox fine Brer Rabbit mixt up wid de Tar-Baby, he feel mighty good, en he roll on de groun' en laff. Bimeby he up'n say, sezee:

"'Well, I speck I got you dis time, Brer Rabbit,

sezee; 'maybe I ain't, but I speck I is. You been runnin' roun' here sassin' atter me a mighty long time, but I speck you done come ter de een' er de row. You bin cuttin' up yo' capers en bouncin' 'roun' in dis neighberhood ontwel you come ter b'leeve yo'se'f de boss er de whole gang. En den youer allers some'rs whar you got no bizness,' sez Brer Fox, sezee. 'Who ax you fer ter come en strike up a 'quaintance wid dish yer Tar-Baby? En who stuck you up dar whar you iz? Nobody in de roun' worril. You des tuck en jam yo'se'f on dat Tar-Baby widout waitin' fer enny invite,' sez Brer Fox, sezee, 'en dar you is, en dar you'll stay twel I fixes up a bresh-pile and fires her up, kaze I'm gwineter bobby-cue you dis day, sho,' sez Brer Fox, sezee.

"Den Brer Rabbit talk mighty 'umble.

"'I don't keer w'at you do wid me, Brer Fox,' sezee, 'so you don't fling me in dat brier-patch. Roas' me, Brer Fox,' sezee, 'but don't fling me in dat brier-patch,' sezee.

"'Hit's so much trouble fer ter kindle a fier,' sez Brer Fox, sezee, 'dat I speck I'll hatter hang you,' sezee.

"'Hang me des ez high as you please, Brer Fox,' sez Brer Rabbit, sezee, 'but do fer de Lord's sake don't fling me in dat brier-patch,' sezee.

"'I ain't got no string,' sez Brer Fox, sezee, 'en now I speck I'll hatter drown you,' sezee.

"'Drown me des ez deep ez you please, Brer Fox,' sez Brer Rabbit, sezee, 'but do don't fling me in dat brier-patch,' sezee.

"'Dey ain't no water nigh,' sez Brer Fox, sezee, 'en now I speck I'll hatter skin you,' sezee.

"'Skin me, Brer Fox,' sez Brer Rabbit, sezee, 'snatch out my eyeballs, t'ar out my years by de roots, en cut off my legs,' sezee, 'but do please, Brer Fox, don't fling me in dat brier-patch,' sezee.

"Co'se Brer Fox wanter hurt Brer Rabbit bad ez
he kin, so he cotch 'im by de behime legs en slung
'im right in de middle er de brier-patch. Dar wuz a

considerbul flutter whar Brer Rabbit struck de
bushes, en Brer Fox sorter hang 'roun' fer ter see w'at
wuz gwineter happen. Bimeby he hear somebody call
'im, en way up de hill he see Brer Rabbit settin' cross-
legged on a chinkapin log koamin' de pitch outen his
har wid a chip. Den Brer Fox know dat he bin swop off
mighty bad. Brer Rabbit wuz bleedzed fer ter fling
back some er his sass, en he holler out:

"'Bred en bawn in a brier-patch, Brer Fox—bred
en bawn in a brier-patch!' en wid dat he skip out des
ez lively ez a cricket in de embers."

V

THE STORY OF THE DELUGE AND HOW IT CAME ABOUT

"ONE time," said Uncle Remus—adjusting his spectacles so as to be able to see how to thread a large darning-needle with which he was patching his coat—"one time, way back yander, 'fo' you wuz borned, honey, en 'fo' Mars John er Miss Sally wuz borned—way back yander 'fo' enny un us wuz borned, de anemils en de creeturs sorter 'lecshuneer roun' 'mong deyselves, twel at las' dey 'greed fer ter have a 'sembly. In dem days," continued the old man, observing

a look of incredulity on the little boy's face, "in dem days creeturs had lots mo' sense dan dey got now;

let 'lone dat, dey had sense same like folks. Hit was
tech en go wid um, too, mon, en w'en dey make up
der mines w'at hatter be done, 'twant mo'n men-
shun'd 'fo' hit wuz done. Well, dey 'lected dat dey
hatter hole er 'sembly fer ter sorter straighten out
marters en hear de complaints, en w'en de day come
dey wuz on han'. De Lion, he wuz dar, kase he wuz
de king, en he hatter be der. De Rhynossyhoss, he
wuz dar, en de Elephent, he wuz dar, en de Cammils,
en de Cows, en plum down ter de Crawfishes, dey
wuz dar. Dey wuz all dar. En w'en de Lion shuck
his mane, en tuck his seat in de big cheer, den de
sesshun begun fer ter commence."

"What did they do, Uncle Remus?" asked the little
boy.

"I can't skacely call to mine 'zackly w'at dey did
do, but dey spoke speeches, en hollered, en cusst, en
flung der langwidge 'roun' des like w'en yo' daddy
wuz gwineter run fer de legislater en got lef'. How-
somever, dey 'ranged der 'fairs, en splained der bizness. Bimeby, w'ile dey wuz 'sputin' 'longer one er
nudder, de Elephent trompled on one er de Crawfishes. Co'se w'en dat creetur put his foot down,
w'atsumever's under dar wuz boun' fer ter be
squshed, en dey wa'n't nuff er dat Crawfish lef' fer
ter tell dat he'd bin dar.

"Dis make de udder Crawfishes mighty mad, en
dey sorter swarmed tergedder en draw'd up a kinder

peramble wid some wharfo'es in it, en read her out in
de 'sembly. But, bless grashus! sech a racket wuz a
gwine on dat nobody ain't hear it, 'ceppin may be de
Mud Turkle en de Spring Lizzud, en dere enfloons
wuz pow'ful lackin'.

"Bimeby, w'iles de Nunicorn wuz 'sputin' wid de
Lion, en w'ile de Hyener wuz a laughin' ter hisse'f, de
Elephent squshed anudder one er de Crawfishes, en a
little mo'n he'd er ruint de Mud Turkle. Den de
Crawfishes, w'at dey wuz lef' un um, swarmed tergedder en draw'd up anudder peramble wid sum mo'
wharfo'es; but dey might ez well er sung Ole Dan
Tucker ter a harrycane. De udder creeturs wuz too
busy wid der fussin' fer ter 'spon' unto de Crawfishes.
So dar dey wuz, de Crawfishes, en dey didn't know
w'at minnit wuz gwineter be de nex'; en dey kep' on
gittin madder en madder en skeerder en skeerder,
twel bimeby dey gun de wink ter de Mud Turkle en
de Spring Lizzud, en den dey bo'd little holes in de
groun' en went down outer sight."

"Who did, Uncle Remus?" asked the little boy.

"De Crawfishes, honey. Dey bo'd inter de groun'
en kep' on bo'in twel dey onloost de fountains er de
earf; en de waters squirt out, en riz higher en higher
twel de hills wuz kivvered, en de creeturs wuz all
drownded; en all bekaze dey let on 'mong deyselves
dat dey wuz bigger dan de Crawfishes."

Then the old man blew the ashes from a smoking yam, and proceeded to remove the peeling.

"Where was the ark, Uncle Remus?" the little boy inquired, presently.

"W'ich ark's dat?" asked the old man, in a tone of well-feigned curiosity.

"Noah's ark," replied the child.

"Don't you pester wid ole man Noah, honey. I boun' he tuck keer er dat ark. Dat's w'at he wuz dar fer, en dat's w'at he done. Leas'ways, dat's w'at dey tells me. But don't you bodder longer dat ark, 'ceppin' your mammy fetches it up. Dey mout er bin two deloojes, en den agin dey moutent. Ef dey wuz enny ark in dish yer w'at de Crawfishes brung on, I ain't heern tell un it, en w'en dey ain't no arks 'roun', I ain't got no time fer ter make um en put um in dar. Hit's gittin' yo' bedtime, honey."

VI

MR. RABBIT GROSSLY DECEIVES MR. FOX

ONE evening when the little boy, whose nights with Uncle Remus were as entertaining as those Arabian ones of blessed memory, had finished supper and hurried out to sit with his venerable patron, he found the old man in great glee. Indeed, Uncle Remus was talking and laughing to himself at such a rate that the little boy was afraid he had company. The truth is, Uncle Remus had heard the child coming, and, when the rosy-cheeked chap put his head in at the door, was engaged in a monologue, the burden of which seemed to be—

> "Ole Molly Har',
> W'at you doin' dar,
> Settin' in de cornder
> Smokin' yo' seegyar?"

As a matter of course this vague allusion reminded the little boy of the fact that the wicked Fox was still in pursuit of the Rabbit, and he immediately put his curiosity in the shape of a question.

"Uncle Remus, did the Rabbit have to go clean

away when he got loose from the Tar-Baby?"

"Bless gracious, honey, dat he didn't. Who? Him? You dunno nuthin' 'tall 'bout Brer Rabbit ef dat's de way you puttin' 'im down. W'at he gwine 'way fer? He moughter stayed sorter close twel de pitch rub off'n his ha'r, but tweren't menny days 'fo' he wuz lopin' up en down de neighborhood same ez ever, en I dunno ef he weren't mo' sassier dan befo'.

"Seem like dat de tale 'bout how he got mixt up wid de Tar-Baby got 'roun' 'mongst de nabers. Leas'-ways, Miss Meadows en de gals got win' un' it, en de nex' time Brer Rabbit paid um a visit Miss Meadows tackled 'im 'bout it, en de gals sot up a monstus gigglement. Brer Rabbit, he sot up des ez cool ez a cowcumber, he did, en let 'em run on."

"Who was Miss Meadows, Uncle Remus?" inquired the little boy.

"Don't ax me, honey. She wuz in de tale, Miss Meadows en de gals wuz, en de tale I give you like hi't wer' gun ter me. Brer Rabbit, he sot dar, he did, sorter lam' like, en den bimeby he cross his legs, he did, and wink his eye slow, en up and say, sezee:

" 'Ladies, Brer Fox wuz my daddy's ridin'-hoss fer thirty year; maybe mo', but thirty year dat I knows un,' sezee; en den he paid um his 'specks, en tip his beaver, en march off, he did, des ez stiff en ez stuck up ez a fire-stick.

"Nex' day, Brer Fox cum a callin', and w'en he gun

fer ter laugh 'bout Brer Rabbit, Miss Meadows en de gals, dey ups en tells 'im 'bout w'at Brer Rabbit say. Den Brer Fox grit his tushes sho' nuff, he did, en he look mighty dumpy, but w'en he riz fer ter go he up en say, sezee:

" 'Ladies, I ain't 'sputin' w'at you say, but I'll make Brer Rabbit chaw up his words en spit um out right yer whar you kin see 'im,' sezee, en wid dat off Brer Fox put.

"En w'en he got in de big road, he shuck de dew off'n his tail, en made a straight shoot fer Brer Rabbit's house. W'en he got dar, Brer Rabbit wuz spectin' un 'im, en de do' wuz shet fas'. Brer Fox knock. Nobody ain't ans'er. Brer Fox knock.

Nobody ans'er. Den he knock agin—blam! blam! Den Brer Rabbit holler out mighty weak:

"'Is dat you, Brer Fox? I want you ter run en fetch de doctor. Dat bait er pusly w'at I e't dis mawnin' is gittin' 'way wid me. Do, please, Brer Fox, run quick,' sez Brer Rabbit, sezee.

"'I come atter you, Brer Rabbit,' sez Brer Fox, sezee. 'Dar's gwineter be a party up at Miss Meadows's,' sezee. 'All de gals 'll be dere, en I promus' dat I'd fetch you. De gals, dey 'lowed dat hit wouldn't be no party 'ceppin' I fotch you,' sez Brer Fox, sezee.

"Den Brer Rabbit say he wuz too sick, en Brer Fox say he wuzzent, en dar dey had it up and down, 'sputin' en contendin'. Brer Rabbit say he can't walk. Brer Fox say he tote 'im. Brer Rabbit say how? Brer Fox say in his arms. Brer Rabbit say he drap 'im. Brer Fox 'low he won't. Bimeby Brer Rabbit say he go ef Brer Fox tote 'im on his back. Brer Fox say he would. Brer Rabbit say he can't ride widout a saddle. Brer Fox say he git de saddle. Brer Rabbit say he can't set in saddle less he have bridle fer ter hol' by. Brer Fox say he git de bridle. Brer Rabbit say he can't ride widout bline bridle, kaze Brer Fox be shyin' at stumps 'long de road, en fling 'im off. Brer Fox say he git bline bridle. Den Brer Rabbit say he go. Den Brer Fox say he ride Brer Rabbit mos' up ter Miss Meadows's, en den he could git down en walk de balance er de way. Brer Rabbit 'greed, en den Brer Fox lipt out atter de saddle en de bridle.

"Co'se Brer Rabbit know de game dat Brer Fox wuz fixin' fer ter play, en he 'termin' fer ter outdo 'im, en by de time he koam his ha'r en twis' his mustarsh, en sorter rig up, yer come Brer Fox, saddle en bridle

on, en lookin' ez peart ez a circus pony. He trot up ter de do' en stan' dar pawin' de ground en chompin' de bit same like sho 'nuff hoss, en Brer Rabbit he mount, he did, en dey amble off. Brer Fox can't see behime wid de bline bridle on, but bimeby he feel Brer Rabbit raise one er his foots.

" 'W'at you doin' now, Brer Rabbit?' sezee.

"Short'nin' de lef stir'p, Brer Fox,' sezee.

"Bimeby Brer Rabbit raise up de udder foot.

" 'W'at you doin' now, Brer Rabbit?' sezee.

" 'Pullin' down my pants, Brer Fox,' sezee.

"All de time, bless grashus, honey, Brer Rabbit wer puttin' on his spurrers, en w'en dey got close to Miss Meadows's, whar Brer Rabbit wuz to git off, en Brer Fox made a motion fer ter stan' still, Brer Rabbit slap de spurrers into Brer Fox flanks, en you better b'leeve he got over groun'. W'en dey got ter de house, Miss Meadows en all de gals wuz settin' on de peazzer, en stidder stoppin' at de gate, Brer Rabbit rid on by, he did, en den come gallopin' down de road en up ter de hoss-rack, w'ich he hitch Brer Fox at, en den he santer inter de house, he did, en shake han's wid de gals, en set dar, smokin' his seegyar same ez a town man. Bimeby he draw in a long puff, en den let hit out in a cloud, en squar hisse'f back en holler out, he did:

" 'Ladies, ain't I done tell you Brer Fox wuz de ridin'-hoss fer our fambly? He sorter losin' his gait now, but I speck I kin fetch 'im all right in a mont' er so,' sezee.

"En den Brer Rabbit sorter grin, he did, en de gals giggle, en Miss Meadows, she praise up de pony, en dar wuz Brer Fox hitch fas' ter de rack, en couldn't he'p hisse'f."

"Is that all," Uncle Remus?" asked the little boy as the old man paused.

"Dat ain't all, honey, but 'twon't do fer ter give out too much cloff fer ter cut one pa'r pants," replied the old man sententiously.

VII

MR. FOX IS AGAIN VICTIMIZED

WHEN "Miss Sally's" little boy went to Uncle Remus the next night to hear the conclusion of the adventure in which the Rabbit made a riding-horse of the Fox to the great enjoyment and gratification of Miss Meadows and the girls, he found the old man in a bad humor.

"I ain't tellin' no tales ter bad chilluns," said Uncle Remus curtly.

"But, Uncle Remus, I ain't bad," said the little boy plaintively.

"Who dat chunkin' dem chickens dis mawnin'? Who dat knockin' out fokes's eyes wid dat Yallerbammer sling des 'fo' dinner? Who dat sickin' dat pinter puppy atter my pig? Who dat scatterin' my ingun sets? Who dat flingin' rocks on top er my house, w'ich a little mo' en one un em would er drap spang on my head?"

"Well, now, Uncle Remus, I didn't go to do it. I won't do so any more. Please, Uncle Remus, if you

will tell me, I'll run to the house and bring you some
tea-cakes."

"Seein' um's better'n hearin' tell un um," replied
the old man, the severity of his countenance relaxing
somewhat; but the little boy darted out, and in a few
minutes came running back with his pockets full and
his hands full.

"I lay yo' mammy 'll 'spishun dat de rats' stummucks is widenin' in dis neighborhood w'en she come
fer ter count up 'er cakes," said Uncle Remus, with a
chuckle. "Deze," he continued, dividing the cakes into
two equal parts—"dese I'll tackle now, en dese I'll lay
by fer Sunday.

"Lemme see. I mos' dis'member wharbouts Brer
Fox en Brer Rab-
bit wuz."

"The rabbit rode
the fox to Miss
Meadows's, and
hitched him to the
horse-rack," said
the little boy.

"W'y co'se he
did," said Uncle
Remus. "C'ose he
did. Well, Brer

Rabbit rid Brer Fox up, he did, en tied 'im to de
rack, en den sot out in de peazzer wid de gals a

smokin' er his seegyar wid mo' proudness dan w'at
you mos' ever see. Dey talk, en dey sing, en dey
play on de peanner, de gals did, twel bimeby hit
come time fer Brer Rabbit fer to be gwine, en he
tell um all good-by, en strut out to de hoss-rack
same's ef he wuz de king er de patter-rollers,* en
den he mount Brer Fox en ride off.

"Brer Fox ain't sayin' nuthin' 'tall. He des rack
off, he did, en keep his mouf shet, en Brer Rabbit
know'd der wuz bizness cookin' up fer him, en he
feel monstus skittish. Brer Fox amble on twel he git
in de long lane, outer sight er Miss Meadows's house,
en den he tu'n loose, he did. He rip en he ra'r, en he
cuss, en he swar; he snort en he cavort."

"What was he doing that for, Uncle Remus?" the
little boy inquired.

"He wuz tryin' fer ter fling Brer Rabbit off'n his
back, bless yo' soul! But he des might ez well er
rastle wid his own shadder. Every time he hump
hisse'f Brer Rabbit slap de spurrers in 'im, en dar dey
had it, up en down. Brer Fox fa'rly to' up de groun'
he did, en he jump so high en he jump so quick dat
he mighty nigh snatch his own tail off. Dey kep' on

---

* Patrols. In the country districts, order was kept on the plantations at night by the knowledge that they were liable to be
visited at any moment by the patrols. Hence a song current among
the negroes, the chorus of which was:

"Run, nigger, run; patter-roller ketch you—
Run, nigger, run; hit's almos' day."

gwine on dis way twel bimeby Brer Fox lay down en
roll over, he did, en dis sorter onsettle Brer Rabbit,
but by de time Brer Fox
got back on his footses
agin, Brer Rabbit wuz
gwine thoo de underbresh
mo' samer dan a race-hoss.
Brer Fox he lit out atter
'im, he did, en he push
Brer Rabbit so close dat it
wuz 'bout all he could do
fer ter git in a holler tree.
Hole too little fer Brer
Fox fer ter git in, en he
hatter lay down en res
en gedder his mine tergedder.

"While he wuz layin'
dar, Mr. Buzzard come
floppin'
'long, en
seein' Brer
Fox stretch
out on de

groun', he lit en view de premusses. Den Mr. Buzzard sorter shake his wing, en put his head on one side, en say to hisse'f like, sezee:

" 'Brer Fox dead, en I so sorry,' sezee.

" 'No I ain't dead, nudder,' sez Brer Fox, sezee. "I got ole man Rabbit pent up in yer,' sezee, 'en I'm a gwine ter git 'im dis time ef it take twel Chris'mus,' sezee.

"Den, atter some mo' palaver, Brer Fox make a bargain dat Mr. Buzzard wuz ter watch de hole, en keep Brer Rabbit dar wiles Brer Fox went atter his axe. Den Brer Fox, he lope off, he did, en Mr. Buzzard, he tuck up his stan' at de hole. Bimeby, w'en all git still, Brer Rabbit sorter scramble down close ter de hole, he did, en holler out:

" 'Brer Fox! Oh! Brer Fox!'

"Brer Fox done gone, en nobody say nuthin'. Den Brer Rabbit squall out like he wuz mad; sezee:

" 'You needn't talk less you wanter,' sezee; 'I knows youer dar, en I ain't keerin',' sezee. 'I des wanter tell you dat I wish mighty bad Brer Tukkey Buzzard wuz here,' sezee.

"Den Mr. Buzzard try ter talk like Brer Fox:

" 'W'at you want wid Mr. Buzzard?' sezee.

" 'Oh, nuthin' in 'tickler, 'cep' dere's de fattes' gray squir'l in yer dat ever I see,' sezee, 'en ef Brer Tukkey Buzzard wuz 'roun' he'd be mighty glad fer ter git 'im,' sezee.

" 'How Mr. Buzzard gwine ter git 'im?' sez de
Buzzard, sezee.

" 'Well, dar's a little hole roun' on de udder side
er de tree,' sez Brer Rabbit, sezee, 'en ef Brer Tukkey

Buzzard wuz here so he could take up his stan' dar,'
sezee, 'I'd drive dat squir'l out,' sezee.

" 'Drive 'im out, den,' sez Mr. Buzzard, sezee, 'en
I'll see dat Brer Tukkey Buzzard gits 'im,' sezee.

"Den Brer Rabbit kick up a racket, like he wer'
drivin' sumpin' out, en Mr. Buzzard he rush 'roun'
fer ter ketch de squir'l, en Brer Rabbit, he dash out,
he did, en he des fly fer home."

At this point Uncle Remus took one of the tea-cakes, held his head back, opened his mouth, dropped the cake in with a sudden motion, looked at the little boy with an expression of astonishment, and then closed his eyes, and begun to chew, mumbling as an accompaniment the plaintive tune of "Don't you Grieve atter Me."

The *séance* was over; but, before the little boy went into the "big house," Uncle Remus laid his rough hand tenderly on the child's shoulder, and remarked, in a confidential tone:

"Honey, you mus' git up soon Chris'mus mawnin' en open de do'; kase I'm gwineter bounce in on Marse John en Miss Sally, en holler Chris'mus gif' des like I useter endurin' de farmin' days fo' de war, w'en ole Miss wuz 'live. I bound' dey don't fergit de ole nigger, nudder. W'en you hear me callin' de pigs, honey, you des hop up en onfassen de do'. I lay I'll give Marse John one er dese yer 'sprize parties."

VIII

MR. FOX IS "OUTDONE" BY MR. BUZZARD

"Ef I don't run inter no mistakes," remarked Uncle Remus, as the little boy came tripping in to see him after supper, "Mr. Tukkey Buzzard wuz gyardin' de holler whar Brer Rabbit went in at, en w'ich he come out un."

The silence of the little boy verified the old man's recollection.

"Well, Mr. Buzzard, he feel mighty lonesome, he did, but he done prommust Brer Fox dat he'd stay, en he 'termin' fer ter sorter hang 'roun' en jine in de joke. En he ain't hatter wait long, nudder, kase bime.

by yer come Brer Fox gallopin' thoo de woods wid his axe on his shoulder.

"'How you speck Brer Rabbit gittin' on, Brer Buzzard?' sez Brer Fox, sezee.

"'Oh, he in dar,' sez Brer Buzzard, sezee. 'He mighty still, dough. I speck he takin' a nap,' sezee.

"'Den I'm des in time fer ter wake 'im up,' sez Brer Fox, sezee. En wid dat he fling off his coat, en spit in his han's, en grab de axe. Den he draw back en come down on de tree—pow! En eve'y time he come down wid de axe—pow!—Mr. Buzzard, he step high, he did, en holler out:

"'Oh, he in dar, Brer Fox. He in dar, sho.'

"En eve'y time a chip ud fly off, Mr. Buzzard, he'd jump, en dodge, en hole his head sideways, he would, en holler:

"'He in dar, Brer Fox. I done heerd 'im. He in dar, sho.'

"En Brer Fox, he lammed away at dat holler tree, he did, like a man maulin' rails, twel bimeby, atter he done got de tree mos' cut thoo, he stop fer ter ketch his bref, en he seed Mr. Buzzard laughin' behime his back, he did, en right den en dar, widout gwine enny fudder, Brer Fox, he smelt a rat. But Mr. Buzzard, he keep on holler'n:

"'He in dar, Brer Fox. He in dar, sho. I done seed 'im.'

"Den Brer Fox, he make like he peepin' up de holler, en he say, sezee:

"'Run yer, Brer Buzzard, en look ef dis ain't Brer Rabbit's foot hanging down yer.'

"En Mr. Buzzard, he come steppin' up, he did,

same ez ef he wer treddin' on kurkle-burs, en he stick
his head in de hole; en no sooner did he done dat dan
Brer Fox grab 'im. Mr. Buzzard flap his wings, en
scramble 'roun' right smartually, he did, but 'twant
no use. Brer Fox had de 'vantage er de grip, he did,
en he hilt 'im right down ter de groun'. Den Mr.
Buzzard squall out, sezee:

"'Lemme 'lone, Brer Fox. Tu'n me loose,' sezee;
'Brer Rabbit'll git out. Youer gittin' close at 'im,'
sezee, 'en leb'm mo' licks'll fetch 'im,' sezee.

"'I'm nigher ter you, Brer Buzzard,' sez Brer Fox,
sezee, 'dan I'll be ter Brer Rabbit dis day,' sezee.
'Wa't you fool me fer?' sezee.

"'Lemme 'lone, Brer Fox,' sez Mr. Buzzard, sezee;
'my ole 'oman waitin' fer me. Brer Rabbit in dar,'
sezee.

"'Dar's a bunch er his fur on dat black-be'y bush,'
sez Brer Fox, sezee, 'en dat ain't de way he come,'
sezee.

"Den Mr. Buzzard up'n tell Brer Fox how 'twuz,
en he low'd, Mr. Buzzard did, dat Brer Rabbit wuz
de lowdownest w'atsizname w'at he ever run up
wid. Den Brer Fox say, sezee:

"'Dat's needer here ner dar, Brer Buzzard,' sezee.
'I lef' you yer fer ter watch dish yere hole, en I lef'
Brer Rabbit in dar. I comes back en I fines you at de
'ole en Brer Rabbit ain't in dar,' sezee. 'I'm gwineter
make you pay fer't. I done bin tampered wid twel

plum' down ter de sap sucker'll set on a log en sassy me. I'm gwinter fling you in a bresh-heap en burn you up,' sezee.

"'Ef you fling me on der fier, Brer Fox, I'll fly 'way,' sez Mr. Buzzard, sezee.

"'Well, den, I'll settle yo' hash right now,' sez Brer Fox, sezee, en wid dat he grab Mr. Buzzard by de tail, he did, en make fer ter dash 'im 'gin de groun', but des 'bout dat time de tail fedders come out, en Mr. Buzzard sail off like one er dese yer berloons; en ez he riz, he holler back:

"'You gimme good start, Brer Fox,' sezee, en Brer Fox sot dar en watch 'im fly outer sight."

"But what became of the Rabbit, Uncle Remus?" asked the little boy.

"Don't you pester 'longer Brer Rabbit, honey, en don't you fret 'bout 'im. You'll year whar he went en how he come out. Dish yer cole snap rastles wid my bones, now," continued the old man, putting on his hat and picking up his walking-stick. "Hit rastles wid me monstus, en I gotter rack 'roun' en see if I kin run up agin some Chris'mus leavin's."

IX

MISS COW FALLS A VICTIM TO MR. RABBIT

"Uncle Remus," said the little boy, "what became of the Rabbit after he fooled the Buzzard, and got out of the hollow tree?"

"Who? Brer Rabbit? Bless yo' soul, honey, Brer Rabbit went skippin' 'long home, he did, des ez sassy ez a jay-bird at a sparrer's nes'. He went gallopin' 'long, he did, but he feel mighty tired ovt, en stiff in his jints, en he wuz mighty nigh dead fcr sumpin fer ter drink, en bimeby, w'en he got mos' home, he spied ole Miss Cow feedin' roun' in a fiel', he did, en he 'termin' fer ter try his han' wid 'er. Brer Rabbit know mighty well dat Miss Cow won't give 'im no milk, kaze she done 'fuse 'im mo'n once, en w'en his ole 'oman wuz sick, at dat. But never mind dat. Brer Rabbit sorter dance up 'long side er de fence, he did, en holler out:

"'Howdy, Sis Cow,' sez Brer Rabbit, sezee.

"'W'y, howdy, Brer Rabbit,' sez Miss Cow, sez she.

"'How you fine yo'se'f deze days, Sis Cow?' sez Brer Rabbit, sezee.

"'I'm sorter toler'ble, Brer Rabbit; how you come on?' sez Miss Cow, sez she.

"'Oh, I'm des toler'ble myse'f, Sis Cow; sorter lin-ger'n' twix' a bauk en a break-down,' sez Brer Rabbit, sezee.

"'How yo' fokes, Brer Rabbit?' sez Miss Cow, sez she.

"'Dey er des middlin', Sis Cow; how Brer Bull gittin' on?' sez Brer Rabbit, sezee.

"'Sorter so-so,' sez Miss Cow, sez she.

"'Dey er some mighty nice 'simmons up dis tree, Sis Cow,' sez Brer Rabbit, sezee, 'en I'd like mighty well fer ter have some un um,' sezee.

"'How you gwineter git um, Brer Rabbit?' sez she.

"'I 'lowed maybe dat I might ax you fer ter butt 'gin de tree, en shake some down, Sis Cow,' sez Brer Rabbit, sezee.

"C'ose Miss Cow don't wanter diskommerdate Brer Rabbit, en she march up ter de 'simmon tree, she did, en hit it a rap wid'er horns—blam! Now, den," continued Uncle Remus, tearing off the corner of a plug of tobacco and cramming it into his mouth— "now, den, dem 'simmons wuz green ez grass, en na'er one never drap. Den Miss Cow butt de tree— blim! Na'er 'simmon drap. Den Miss Cow sorter back off little, en run agin de tree—blip! No 'sim-mons never drap. Den Miss Cow back off little fud-der, she did, en hi'st her tail on 'er back, en come agin de tree, kerblam! en she come so fas', en she come so hard, twel one 'er her horns went spang thoo de tree, en dar she wuz. She can't go forreds, en she can't go backerds. Dis zackly w'at Brer Rabbit waitin' fer, en he no sooner seed ole Miss Cow all fas'en'd up dan he jump up, he did, en cut de pidjin-wing.

"'Come he'p me out, Brer Rabbit,' sez Miss Cow, sez she.

"'I can't clime, Sis Cow,' sez Brer Rabbit, sezee, 'but I'll run'n tell Brer Bull,' sezee; en wid dat Brer Rabbit put out fer home, en 'twan't long 'fo here he come wid his ole 'oman en all his chilluns, en de las' one er de fambly wuz totin' a pail. De big uns had big pails, en de little uns had little pails. En dey all s'roundid ole Miss Cow, dey did, en you hear me, honey, dey milk't 'er dry. De ole uns milk't en de young uns milk't, en den w'en dey done got nuff, Brer Rabbit, he up'n say, sezee:

"'I wish you mighty well, Sis Cow. I 'low'd bein's how dat you'd hatter sorter camp out all night dat I'd better come en swaje yo' bag,' sezee."

"Do which, Uncle Remus?" asked the little boy.

"Go 'long, honey! Swaje 'er bag. W'en cows don't git milk't, der bag swells, en youk'n hear um a moanin' en a beller'n des like dey wuz gittin' hurtid. Dat's w'at Brer Rabbit done. He 'sembled his fambly, he did, en he swaje ole Miss Cow's bag.

"Miss Cow, she stood dar, she did, en she study en study, en strive fer ter break loose, but de horn done bin jam in de tree so tight dat twuz way 'fo day in de mornin' 'fo' she loose it. Anyhow hit wuz endurin' er de night, en atter she git loose she sorter graze 'roun', she did, fer ter jestify 'er stummuck she 'low'd, ole Miss Cow did, dat Brer Rabbit be hoppin' 'long dat way fer ter see how she gittin' on, en she tuck'n lay er trap fer 'im; en des 'bout sunrise wat'd ole Miss Cow do but march up ter de 'simmon tree en stick er horn back in de hole? But, bless yo' soul, honey, w'ile she wuz croppin' de grass she tuck one moufull too menny, kaze w'en she hitch on ter de 'simmon tree agin, Brer Rabbit wuz settin' in de fence cornder a watchin' un 'er. Den Brer Rabbit he say ter hisse'f:

"'Heyo,' sezee, 'w'at dis yer gwine on now? Hole

yo' hosses, Sis Cow, twel you hear me comin',' sezee.

"En den he crope off down de fence, Brer Rabbit did, en bimeby here he come—lippity-clippity, clippity-lippity—des a sailin' down de big road.

"'Mornin', Sis Cow,' sez Brer Rabbit, sezee, 'how you come on dis mornin'?' sezee.

"'Po'ly, Brer Rabbit, po'ly,' sez Miss Cow, sez she. 'I ain't had no res' all night,' sez she. 'I can't pull loose,' sez she, 'but ef you'll come en ketch holt er my tail, Brer Rabbit,' sez she, 'I reckin may be I kin fetch my horn out,' sez she. Den Brer Rabbit, he come up little closer, but he ain't gittin' too close.

"'I speck I'm nigh nuff, Sis Cow,' sez Brer Rabbit, sezee. 'I'm a mighty puny man, en I might git trompled,' sezee. 'You do de pullin', Sis Cow,' sezee, 'en I'll do de gruntin',' sezee.

"Den Miss Cow, she pull out 'er horn, she did, en tuck atter Brer Rabbit, en down de big road dey had it, Brer Rabbit wid his years laid back, en Miss Cow wid 'er head down en 'er tail curl. Brer Rabbit kep' on gainin', en bimeby he dart in a brier-patch, en by de time Miss Cow come 'long he had his head stickin' out, en his eyes look big ez Miss Sally's chany sassers.

"'Heyo, Sis Cow! Whar you gwine?' sez Brer Rabbit, sezee.

"'Howdy, Brer Big-Eyes,' sez Miss Cow, sez she. 'Is you seed Brer Rabbit go by?'

"'He des dis minit pass,' sez Brer Rabbit, sezee, 'en he look mighty sick,' sezee.

"En wid dat, Miss Cow tuck down de road like de dogs wuz atter 'er, en Brer Rabbit, he des lay down dar in de brier-patch en roll en laugh twel his sides hurtid 'im. He bleedzd ter laff. Fox atter 'im, Buzzard atter 'im, en Cow atter 'im, en dey ain't kotch 'im yit."

X

MR. TERRAPIN APPEARS UPON THE SCENE

"Miss Sally's" little boy again occupying the anxious position of auditor, Uncle Remus took the shovel and "put de noses er de chunks tergedder," as he expressed it, and then began:

"One day, atter Sis Cow done run pas' 'er own shadder tryin' fer ter ketch 'im. Brer Rabbit tuck'n 'low dat he wuz gwineter drap in en see Miss Meadows en de gals, en he got out his piece er lookin'-glass en primp up, he did, en sot out. Gwine canterin' 'long de road, who should Brer Rabbit run up wid

but ole Brer Tarrypin—de same ole one-en-sixpunce.
Brer Rabbit stop, he did, en rap on de roof er Brer
Tarrypin house."

"On the roof of his house, Uncle Remus?" interrupted the little boy.

"Co'se honey, Brer Tarrypin kare his house wid
'im. Rain er shine, hot er cole, strike up wid ole Brer

Tarrypin w'en you will en w'ilst you may, en whar
you fine 'im, dar you'll fine his shanty. Hit's des like
I tell you. So den! Brer Rabbit he rap on de roof er
Brer Tarrypin's house, he did, en ax wuz he in, en
Brer Tarrypin 'low dat he wuz, en den Brer Rabbit,

he ax 'im howdy, en den Brer Tarrypin he likewise
'spon' howdy, en den Brer Rabbit he say whar wuz
Brer Tarrypin gwine, en Brer Tarrypin, he say w'ich
he wern't gwine nowhar skasely. Den Brer Rabbit
'low he wuz on his way fer ter see Miss Meadows en
de gals, en he ax Brer Tarrypin ef he won't jine in en
go long, en Brer Tarrypin 'spon' he don't keer ef he
do, en den dey sot out. Dey had plenty er time fer
confabbin' 'long de way, but bimeby dey got dar, en
Miss Meadows en de gals dey come ter de do', dey
did, en ax um in, en in dey went.

"W'en dey got in, Brer Tarrypin wuz so flat-footed
dat he wuz too low on de flo', en he wern't high nuff
in a cheer, but while dey wuz all scrambling' 'roun'
tryin' fer ter git Brer Tarrypin a cheer, Brer Rabbit,
he pick 'im up en put 'im on de shelf whar de water-
bucket sot, en ole Brer Tarrypin, he lay back up dar,
he did, des es proud ez a nigger wid a cook 'possum.

"Co'se de talk fell on Brer Fox, en Miss Meadows
en de gals make a great 'miration 'bout w'at a gaily
ridin'-hoss Brer Fox wuz, en dey make lots er fun, en
laugh en giggle same like gals duz deze days. Brer
Rabbit, he sot dar in de cheer smokin' his seegyar, en
he sorter kler up his th'oat, en say, sezee:

"'I'd er rid 'im over dis mawnin', ladies,' sezee,
'but I rid 'im so hard yistiddy dat he went lame in
de off fo' leg, en I speck I'll hatter swop 'im off yit,'
sezee.

"Den Brer Tarrypin, he up'n say, sezee:

"'Well, ef you gwinter sell 'im, Brer Rabbit,' sezee, 'sell him some'rs outen dis naberhood, kase he done bin yer too long now,' sezee. 'No longer'n day 'fo' yistiddy,' sezee, 'Brer Fox pass me on de road, en whatter you reckin he say?' sezee:

"'Law, Brer Tarrypin,' sez Miss Meadows, sez she, 'you don't mean ter say he cust?' sez she, en den de gals hilt der fans up 'fo' der faces.

"'Oh, no, ma'm,' sez Brer Tarrypin, sezee, 'he didn't cust, but he holler out—"Heyo, Stinkin' Jim!"' sezee.

"'Oh, my! You hear dat, gals?' sez Miss Meadows,

sez she; 'Brer Fox call Brer Tarrypin Stinkin' Jim,' sez she, en den Miss Meadows en de gals make great

wonderment how Brer Fox kin talk dat a way 'bout
nice man like Brer Tarrypin.

"But bless grashus, honey! w'ilst all dis gwine on,
Brer Fox wuz stannin' at de back do' wid one year at
de cat-hole lissenin'. Eave-drappers don't hear no
good er deyse'f, en de way Brer Fox wuz 'bused dat
day wuz a caution.

"Bimeby Brer Fox stick his head in de do', en
holler out:

"'Good evenin', fokes, I wish you mighty well,'
sezee, en wid dat he make a dash for Brer Rabbit, but
Miss Meadows en de gals dey holler en squall, dey
did, en Brer Tarrypin he got ter scramblin' roun' up
dar on de shelf, en off he come, en blip he tuck Brer
Fox on de back er de head. Dis sorter stunted Brer
Fox, en w'en he gedder his 'membunce de mos' he
seed wuz a pot er greens turnt over in de fireplace, en
a broke cheer. Brer Rabbit wuz gone, en Brer Tarrypin wuz gone, en Miss Meadows en de gals wuz
gone."

"Where did the Rabbit go, Uncle Remus?" the
little boy asked, after a pause.

"Bless yo' soul, honey! Brer Rabbit he skint up de
chimbly—dats w'at turnt de pot er greens over. Brer
Tarrypin, he crope under de bed, he did, en got
behime de cloze-chist, en Miss Meadows en de gals,
dey run out in de yard.

"Brer Fox, he sorter look roun' en feel er de back

er his head, whar Brer Tarrypin lit, but he don't see no sine er Brer Rabbit. But de smoke en de ashes gwine up de chimbly got de best er Brer Rabbit, en bimeby he sneeze—*huckychow!*

"'Aha!' sez Brer Fox, sezee; 'youer dar, is you?' sezee. 'Well, I'm gwineter smoke you out, ef it takes

a mont'. Youer mine dis time,' sezee. Brer Rabbit ain't sayin' nuthin'.

"'Ain't you comin' down?' sez Brer Fox, sezee. Brer Rabbit ain't sayin' nuthin'. Den Brer Fox, he went out atter some wood, he did, en w'en he come back he hear Brer Rabbit laughin'.

"'W'at you laughin' at, Brer Rabbit?' sez Brer Fox, sezee.

"'Can't tell you, Brer Fox,' sez Brer Rabbit, sezee.

"'Better tell, Brer Rabbit,' sez Brer Fox, sezee.

"''Tain't nuthin' but a box er money somebody done gone en lef' up yer in de chink er de chimbly,' sez Brer Rabbit, sezee.

"'Don't b'leeve you,' sez Brer Fox, sezee.

"'Look up en see,' sez Brer Rabbit, sezee, en w'en Brer Fox look up, Brer Rabbit spit his eyes full er terbarker joose, he did, en Brer Fox, he make a break fer de branch, en Brer Rabbit he come down en tole de ladies good-by.

"'How you git 'im off, Brer Rabbit?' sez Miss Meadows, sez she.

"'Who? me?' sez Brer Rabbit, sezee; 'w'y I des tuck en tole 'im dat ef he didn't go 'long home en stop playin' his pranks on spectubble fokes, dat I'd take 'im out and th'ash 'im,' sezee."

"And what became of the Terrapin?" asked the little boy.

"Oh, well den!" exclaimed the old man, "chilluns can't speck ter know all 'bout eve'ything 'fo' dey git some res'. Dem eyeleds er yone wanter be propped wid straws dis minnit."

XI

MR. WOLF MAKES A FAILURE

"I LAY yo' ma got comp'ny," said Uncle Remus, as the little boy entered the old man's door with a huge piece of mince-pie in his hand, 'en ef she ain't got comp'ny, den she done gone en drap de cubberd key som'ers whar you done run up wid it."

"Well, I saw the pie lying there, Uncle Remus, and I just thought I'd fetch it out to you."

"Tooby sho, honey," replied the old man, regarding the child with admiration. "Tooby sho, honey; dat changes marters. Chrismus doin's is outer date, en dey ain't got no bizness layin' roun' loose. Dish yer pie," Uncle Remus continued, holding it up and measuring it with an experienced eye, "will gimme strenk fer ter persoo on atter Brer Fox en Brer Rabbit en de udder creeturs w'at dey roped in 'long wid um."

Here the old man paused, and proceeded to demolish the pie—a feat accomplished in a very short time. Then he wiped the crumbs from his beard and began:

"Brer Fox feel so bad, en he git so mad 'bout Brer Rabbit, dat he dunner w'at ter do, en he look mighty down-hearted. Bimeby, one day wiles he wuz gwine 'long de road, old Brer Wolf come up wid 'im. W'en dey done howdyin' en axin' atter one nudder's fambly

connexshun, Brer Wolf, he 'low, he did, dat der wuz
sump'n wrong wid Brer Fox, en Brer Fox, he 'low'd

der wern't, en he went on en laugh en make great
terdo kaze Brer Wolf look like he spishun sump'n.
But Brer Wolf, he got mighty long head, en he sorter
broach 'bout Brer Rabbit's kyar'ns on, kaze de way
dat Brer Rabbit 'ceive Brer Fox done got ter be de
talk er de naberhood. Den Brer Fox en Brer Wolf dey
sorter palavered on, dey did, twel bimeby Brer Wolf

he up'n say dat he done got plan fix fer ter trap Brer
Rabbit. Den Brer Fox say how. Den Brer Wolf up'n
tell 'im dat de way fer ter git de drap on Brer Rabbit
wuz ter git 'im in Brer Fox house. Brer Fox dun know
Brer Rabbit uv ole, en he know dat sorter game done
wo' ter a frazzle, but Brer Wolf, he talk mighty
'swadin'.

"'How you gwine git 'im dar?' sez Brer Fox, sezee.

"'Fool 'im dar,' sez Brer Wolf, sezee.

"'Who gwine do de foolin'?' sez Brer Fox, sezee.

"'I'll do de foolin',' sez Brer Wolf, sezee, 'ef you'll
do de gamin',' sezee.

"'How you gwine do it?' sez Brer Fox, sezee.

"'You run 'long home, en git on de bed, en make
like you dead, en don't you say nothin' twel Brer
Rabbit come en put his han's onter you,' sez Brer
Wolf, sezee, 'en ef we don't git 'im fer supper, Joe's
dead en Sal's a widder,' sezee.

"Dis look like mighty nice game, en Brer Fox
'greed. So den he amble off home, en Brer Wolf, he
march off ter Brer Rabbit house. W'en he got dar, hit
look like nobody at home, but Brer Wolf he walk up
en knock on de do'—blam! blam! Nobody come. Den
he lam aloose en knock 'gin—blim! blim!

"'Who dar?' sez Brer Rabbit, sezee.

"'Fr'en',' sez Brer Wolf.

"'Too menny fr'en's spiles de dinner,' sez Brer
Rabbit, sezee; 'w'ich un's dis?' sezee

" 'I fetch bad news, Brer Rabbit,' sez Brer Wolf, sezee.

" 'Bad news is soon tole,' sez Brer Rabbit, sezee.

"By dis time Brer Rabbit done come ter de do', wid his head tied up in a red hankcher.

" 'Brer Fox died dis mornin',' sez Brer Wolf, sezee.

" 'Whar yo' mo'nin' gown, Brer Wolf?' sez Brer Rabbit, sezee.

" 'Gwine atter it now,' sez Brer Wolf, sezee. 'I des call by fer ter bring de news. I went down ter Brer

Fox house little bit 'go, en dar I foun' 'im stiff,' sezee.

"Den Brer Wolf lope off. Brer Rabbit sot down en

scratch his head, he did, en bimeby he say ter hisse'f dat he b'leeve he sorter drap 'roun' by Brer Fox house fer ter see how de lan' lay. No sooner said'n done. Up he jump, en out he went. W'en Brer Rabbit got close ter Brer Fox house, all look lonesome. Den he went up nigher. Nobody stirrin'. Den he look in, en dar lay Brer Fox stretch out on de bed des es big ez life. Den Brer Rabbit make like he talkin' to hisse'f.

"'Nobody 'roun' fer ter look atter Brer Fox—not even Brer Tukkey Buzzard ain't come ter de funer'l,' sezee. 'I hope Brer Fox ain't dead, but I speck he is,' sezee. 'Even down ter Brer Wolf done gone en lef' 'im. Hit's de busy season wid me, but I'll set up wid 'im. He seem like he dead, yit he mayn't be,' sez Brer Rabbit, sezee. 'W'en a man go ter see dead fokes, dead fokes allers raises up der behime leg en hollers, *wahoo!*' sezee.

"Brer Fox he stay still. Den Brer Rabbit he talk little louder:

"'Mighty funny. Brer Fox look like he dead, yit he don't do like he dead. Dead fokes hists der behime leg en hollers *wahoo!* w'en a man come ter see um,' sez Brer Rabbit, sezee.

"Sho' nuff, Brer Fox lif' up his foot en holler *wahoo!* en Brer Rabbit he tear out de house like de dogs wuz atter 'im. Brer Wolf mighty smart, but nex' time you hear fum 'im, honey, he'll be in trouble. You des hole yo' breff'n wait."

XII

MR. FOX TACKLES OLD MAN TARRYPIN

"One day," said Uncle Remus, sharpening his knife on the palm of his hand—"one day Brer Fox strike up wid Brer Tarrypin right in de middle er de big road. Brer Tarrypin done heerd 'im comin', en he 'low ter hissef dat he'd sorter keep one eye open; but Brer Fox wuz monstus perlite, en he open up de confab, he did, like he ain't see Brer Tarrypin sence de las' freshit.

"'Heyo, Brer Tarrypin, whar you bin dis long-come-short?' sez Brer Fox, sezee.

"'Lounjun 'roun', Brer Fox, lounjun 'roun',' sez Brer Tarrypin.

" 'You don't look sprucy like you did, Brer Tarry-pin,' sez Brer Fox, sezee.

" 'Lounjun 'roun' en suffer'n', sez Brer Tarrypin, sezee.

"Den de talk sorter run on like dis:

" 'W'at ail you, Brer Tarrypin? Yo' eye look mighty red,' sez Brer Fox, sezee.

" 'Lor', Brer Fox, you dunner w'at trubble is. You ain't bin lounjun 'roun' en suffer'n',' sez Brer Tarry-pin, sezee.

" 'Bofe eyes red, en you look like you mighty weak, Brer Tarrypin,' sez Brer Fox, sezee.

" 'Lor', Brer Fox, you dunner w'at trubble is,' sez Brer Tarrypin, sezee.

" 'W'at ail you now, Brer Tarrypin?' sez Brer Fox, sezee.

" 'Tuck a walk de udder day, en man come 'long en sot de fiel' a-fier. Lor', Brer Fox, you dunner w'at trubble is,' sez Brer Tarrypin, sezee.

" 'How you git out de fier, Brer Tarrypin?' sez Brer Fox, sezee.

" 'Sot en tuck it, Brer Fox,' sez Brer Tarrypin, sezee. 'Sot en tuck it, en de smoke sif' in my eye, en de fier scorch my back,' sez Brer Tarrypin, sezee.

" 'Likewise hit bu'n yo' tail off,' sez Brer Fox, sezee.

" 'Oh, no, dar's de tail, Brer Fox,' sez Brer Tarry-pin, sezee, en wid dat he oncurl his tail fum under de shell, en no sooner did he do dat dan Brer Fox grab it, en holler out:

"'Oh, yes, Brer Tarrypin! Oh, yes! En so youer de man w'at lam me on de head at Miss Meadows's is you? Youer in wid Brer Rabbit, is you? Well, I'm gwineter out you.'

"Brer Tarrypin beg en beg, but 'twan't no use. Brer Fox done been fool so much dat he look like he 'termin' fer ter have Brer Tarrypin haslett. Den Brer Tarrypin beg Brer Fox not fer ter drown 'im, but Brer Fox ain't makin' no prommus, en den he beg Brer Fox fer ter bu'n' 'im, kase he done useter fier, but Brer Fox don't say nuthin'. Bimeby Brer Fox drag Brer Tarrypin off little ways b'low de spring-'ouse, en souze him under de water. Den Brer Tarrypin begin fer ter holler:

"'Tu'n loose dat stump root en ketch holt er me—tu'n loose dat stump root en ketch holt er me.'

"Brer Fox he holler back:

"'I ain't got holt er no stump root, en I is got holt er you.'

"Brer Tarrypin he keep on holler'n:

"'Ketch holt er me—I'm a drownin'—I'm a drownin'—tu'n loose de stump root en ketch holt er me.'

"Sho nuff, Brer Fox tu'n loose de tail, en Brer Tarrypin, he went down ter de bottom—kerblunkity-blink!"

No typographical combination or description could

do justice to the guttural sonorousness—the peculiar intonation—which Uncle Remus imparted to this

combination. It was so peculiar, indeed, that the little boy asked:

"How did he go to the bottom, Uncle Remus?"

"Kerblunkity-blink!"

"Was he drowned, Uncle Remus?"

"Who? Ole man Tarrypin? Is you drowndid w'en yo' ma tucks you in de bed?"

"Well, no," replied the little boy, dubiously.

"Ole man Tarrypin wuz at home I tell you, honey. Kerblinkity-blunk!"

XIII

THE AWFUL FATE OF MR. WOLF

UNCLE REMUS was half-soling one of his shoes, and his Miss Sally's little boy had been handling his awls, his hammers, and his knives to such an extent that the old man was compelled to assume a threatening attitude; but peace reigned again, and the little boy perched himself on a chair, watching Uncle Remus driving in pegs.

"Folks w'at's allers pesterin' people, en bodderin' 'longer dat w'at ain't dern, don't never come ter no good eend. Dar wuz Brer Wolf; stidder mindin' un his own bizness, he hatter take en go in pardnerships wid Brer Fox, en dey want skacely a minnit in de day dat he want atter Brer Rabbit, en he kep' on en kep' on twel fus' news you knowed he got kotch up wid— en he got kotch up wid monstus bad."

"Goodness, Uncle Remus! I thought the Wolf let

the Rabbit alone, after he tried to fool him about the
Fox being dead."

"Better lemme tell dish yer my way. Bimeby hit'll
be yo' bed time, en Miss Sally'll be a hollerin' atter

you, en you'll be a whimplin' roun', en den Mars
John'll fetch up de re'r wid dat ar strop w'at I made
fer 'im."

The child laughed, and playfully shook his fist in
the simple, serious face of the venerable old darkey,
but said no more. Uncle Remus waited awhile to be
sure there was to be no other demonstration, and
then proceeded:

"Brer Rabbit ain't see no peace w'atsumever. He

can't leave home 'cep' Brer Wolf 'ud make a raid en
tote off some er de fambly. Brer Rabbit b'ilt 'im a
straw house, en hit wuz tored down; den he made a
house outen pine-tops, en dat went de same way;
den he made 'im a bark house, en dat wuz raided on,
en eve'y time he los' a house he los' one er his chilluns. Las' Brer Rabbit got mad, he did, en cust, en
den he went off, he did, en got some kyarpinters, en
dey b'ilt 'im a plank house wid rock foundashuns.
Atter dat he could have some peace en quietness.
He could go out en pass de time er day wid his
neighbors, en come back en set by de fier, en smoke
his pipe, en read de newspapers same like enny man
w'at got a fambly. He made a hole, he did, in de
cellar whar de little Rabbits could hide out w'en dar
wuz much uv a racket in de neighborhood, en de
latch er de front do' kotch on de inside. Brer Wolf,
he see how de lan' lay, he did, en he lay low. De
little Rabbits was mighty skittish, but hit got so dat
cole chills ain't run up Brer Rabbit's back no mo' w'en
he heerd Brer Wolf go gallopin' by.

"Bimeby, one day w'en Brer Rabbit wuz fixin' fer
ter call on Miss Coon, he heerd a monstrus fuss en
clatter up de big road, en 'mos' 'fo' he could fix his
years fer ter lissen, Brer Wolf run in de do'. De little
Rabbits dey went inter dere hole in de cellar, dey
did, like blowin' out a cannle. Brer Wolf wuz far'ly
kivver'd wid mud, en mighty nigh outer win'.

"'Oh, do pray save me, Brer Rabbit!' sez Brer
Wolf, sezee. 'Do please, Brer Rabbit! de dogs is
ater me, en dey'll t'ar me up. Don't you year um

comin'? Oh, do please save me, Brer Rabbit! Hide
me some'rs whar de dogs won't git me.'

"No quicker sed dan done.

"'Jump in dat big chist dar, Brer Wolf,' sez Brer
Rabbit, sezee; 'jump in dar en make yo'se'f at
home.'

"In jump Brer Wolf, down come the led, en inter
de hasp went de hook, en dar Mr. Wolf wuz. Den
Brer Rabbit went ter de lookin'-glass, he did, en wink

at hisse'f, en den he draw'd de rockin'-cheer in front
er de fier, he did, en tuck a big chaw terbarker."

"Tobacco, Uncle Remus?" asked the little boy, in-
credulously.

"Rabbit terbarker, honey. You know dis yer life
ev'lastin' w'at Miss Sally puts 'mong de cloze in de
trunk; well, dat's rabbit terbarker. Den Brer Rabbit
sot dar long time, he did, turnin' his mine over en
wukken his thinkin' masheen. Bimeby he got up, en
sorter stir 'roun'. Den Brer Wolf open up:

"'Is de dogs all gone, Brer Rabbit?'

"'Seem like I hear one un um smellin' roun' de
chimbly-cornder des now.'

"Den Brer Rabbit git de kittle en fill it full er
water, en put it on de fier.

"'W'at you doin' now, Brer Rabbit?'

"'I'm fixin fer ter make you a nice cup er tea,
Brer Wolf.'

"Den Brer Rabbit
went ter de cubberd
en git de gimlet, en
commence for ter bo'
little holes in de chist-
led.

"'W'at you doin'
now, Brer Rabbit?'

"'I'm bo'in' little holes so you kin get bref, Brer
Wolf.'

"Den Brer Rabbit went out en git some mo' wood, en fling it on de fier.

" 'W'at you doin' now, Brer Rabbit?'

" 'I'm a chunkin' up de fier so you won't git cole, Brer Wolf.'

"Den Brer Rabbit went down inter de cellar en fotch out all his chilluns.

" 'W'at you doin' now, Brer Rabbit?'

" 'I'm a tellin' my chilluns w'at a nice man you is, Brer Wolf.'

"En de chilluns, dey had ter put der han's on der moufs fer ter keep fum laffin'. Den Brer Rabbit he got de kittle en commenced fer to po' de hot water on de chist-lid.

" 'W'at dat I hear, Brer Rabbit?'

" 'You hear de win' a blowin', Brer Wolf.'

"Den de water begin fer ter sif' thoo.

" 'W'at dat I feel, Brer Rabbit?'

" 'You feels de fleas a bitin', Brer Wolf.'

" 'Dey er bitin' mighty hard, Brer Rabbit.'

" 'Tu'n over on de udder side, Brer Wolf.'

" 'W'at dat I feel now, Brer Rabbit?'

" 'Still you feels de fleas, Brer Wolf.'

" 'Dey er eatin' me up, Brer Rabbit,' en dem wuz de las words er Brer Wolf, kase de scaldin' water done de bizness.

"Den Brer Rabbit call in his neighbors, he did, en dey hilt a reg'lar juberlee; en ef you go ter Brer Rab-

bit's house right now, I dunno but w'at you'll fine
Brer Wolf's hide hangin' in de back-po'ch, en all bekaze he wuz so bizzy wid udder fo'kses doin's."

XIV

MR. FOX AND THE DECEITFUL FROGS

WHEN the little boy ran in to see Uncle Remus the
night after he had told him of the awful fate of Brer
Wolf, the only response to his greeting was:

'I-doom-er-ker-kum-mer-ker!"

No explanation could convey an adequate idea of
the intonation and pronunciation which Uncle Remus
brought to bear upon this wonderful word. Those
who can recall to mind the peculiar gurgling, jerking,
liquid sound made by pouring water from a large jug,
or the sound produced by throwing several stones in
rapid succession into a pond of deep water, may be
able to form a very faint idea of the sound, but it can
not be reproduced in print. The little boy was astonished.

"What did you say, Uncle Remus?"

"I-doom-er-ker-kum-mer-ker! I-doom-er-ker-kum-
mer-ker!"

"What is that?"

"Dat's Tarrypin talk, dat is. Bless yo' soul, honey,"
continued the old man, brightening up, "w'en you git
ole ez me—w'en you see w'at I sees, en year w'at I

years—de creeturs dat you can't talk wid 'll be mighty skase—dey will dat. W'y, ders er old gray rat w'at uses 'bout yer, en time atter time he comes out w'en you all done gone ter bed en sets up dar in de cornder en dozes, en me en him talks by de 'our; en w'at dat old rat dunno ain't down in de spellin' book. Des now, w'en you run in and broke me up, I wuz fetchin'

into my mine w'at Brer Tarrypin say ter Brer Fox w'en he turn 'im loose in de branch."

"What did he say, Uncle Remus?"

"Dat w'at he said—I-doom-er-ker-kum-mer-ker!
Brer Tarrypin wuz at de bottom er de pon', en he talk
back, he did, in bubbles—I-doom-er-ker-kum-mer-ker!
Brer Fox, he ain't sayin' nuthin', but Brer Bull-Frog,

settin' on de bank, he hear Brer Tarrypin, he did, en
he holler back:

" 'Jug-er-rum-kum-dum! Jug-er-rum-kum-dum!'

"Den n'er Frog holler out:

" 'Knee-deep! Knee-deep!'

"Den ole Brer Bull-Frog, he holler back:

" 'Don'-you-ber-lieve-'im! Don't-you-berlieve-'im!'

"Den de bubbles come up fum Brer Tarrypin:

" 'I-doom-er-ker-kum-mer-ker!'

"Den n'er Frog sing out:

" 'Wade in! Wade in!'

"Den ole Brer Bull-Frog talk thoo his ho'seness:

' 'Dar-you'll-fine-yo'-brudder!   Dar-you'll-fine-yo'-brudder!'

"Sho nuff, Brer Fox look over de bank, he did, en dar wuz n'er Fox lookin' at 'im outer de water. Den he retch out fer ter shake han's, en in he went, heels over head, en Brer Tarrypin bubble out:

" 'I-doom-er-ker-kum-mer-ker!' "

"Was the Fox drowned, Uncle Remus?" asked the little boy.

"He weren't zackly drowndid, honey," replied the old man, with an air of cautious reserve. "He did manage fer ter scramble out, but a little mo' en de Mud Turkle would er got 'im, en den he'd er bin made hash un worril widout een'."

XV

MR. FOX GOES A-HUNTING, BUT MR. RABBIT
BAGS THE GAME

"Atter Brer Fox hear 'bout how Brer Rabbit
done Brer Wolf," said Uncle Remus, scratching his
head with the point of his awl, "he 'low, he did, dat
he better not be so brash, en he sorter let Brer Rabbit 'lone. Dey wuz all time seein' one nudder, en
'bunnunce er times Brer Fox could er nab Brer Rabbit, but eve'y time he got de chance, his mine 'ud
sorter rezume 'bout Brer Wolf, en he let Brer Rabbit
'lone. Bimeby dey 'gun ter git kinder familious wid
wunner nudder like dey useter, en it got so Brer
Fox'd call on Brer Rabbit, en dey'd set up en smoke
der pipes, dey would, like no ha'sh feelin's 'd ever
rested 'twixt um.

"Las', one day Brer Fox come 'long all rig out, en
ax Brer Rabbit fer ter go huntin' wid 'im, but Brer
Rabbit, he sorter feel lazy, en he tell Brer Fox dat
he got some udder fish fer ter fry. Brer Fox feel
mighty sorry, he did, but he say he b'leeve he try his
han' enny how, en off he put. He wuz gone all day,
en he had a monstus streak er luck, Brer Fox did, en
he bagged a sight er game. Bimeby, to'rds de shank
er de evenin', Brer Rabbit sorter stretch hisse'f, he
did, en 'low hit's mos' time fer Brer Fox fer ter git

'long home. Den Brer Rabbit, he went'n mounted a
stump fer ter see ef he could year Brer Fox comin'.
He ain't bin dar long, twel sho' nuff, yer come Brer

Fox thoo de woods, singing like a nigger at a frolic.
Brer Rabbit, he lipt down off'n de stump, he did, en
lay down in de road en make like he dead. Brer Fox
he come 'long, he did, en see Brer Rabbit layin' dar.
He tu'n 'im over, he did, en 'zamine 'im, en say,
sezee:

" 'Dish yer rabbit dead. He look like he bin dead
long time. He dead, but he mighty fat. He de fattes'

rabbit w'at I ever see, but he bin dead too long. I
feard ter take 'im home,' sezee.

"Brer Rabbit ain't sayin' nuthin'. Brer Fox, he
sorter lick his chops, but he went on en lef' Brer
Rabbit layin' in de road. Dreckly he wuz outer sight,
Brer Rabbit, he jump up, he did, en run roun' thoo de
woods en git befo Brer Fox agin. Brer Fox, he come
up, en dar lay Brer Rabbit, periently cole en stiff.
Brer Fox, he look at Brer Rabbit, en he sorter study.

Atter while he onslung his game-bag, en say ter
hisse'f, sezee:

"'Deze yer rabbits gwine ter was'e. I'll des 'bout leave my game yer, en I'll go back'n git dat udder rabbit, en I'll make fokes b'leeve dat I'm ole man Hunter fum Huntsville,' sezee.

"En wid dat he drapt his game en loped back up de road atter de udder rabbit, en w'en he got outer sight, ole Brer Rabbit, he snatch up Brer Fox game en put out fer home. Nex' time he see Brer Fox he holler out:

"'What you kill de udder day, Brer Fox?' sezee.

"Den Brer Fox, he sorter koam his flank wid his tongue, en holler back:

"'I kotch a han'ful er hard sense, Brer Rabbit,' sezee.

"Den ole Brer Rabbit, he laff, he did, en up en 'spon', sezee:

"'Ef I'd a know'd you wuz atter dat, Brer Fox, I'd a loant you some er mine,' sezee."

XVI

OLD MR. RABBIT, HE'S A GOOD FISHERMAN

"Brer Rabbit en Brer Fox wuz like some chilluns w'at I knows un," said Uncle Remus, regarding the little boy, who had come to hear another story, with an affectation of great solemnity. "Bofe un um wuz allers atter wunner nudder, a prankin' en a pester'n 'roun', but Brer Rabbit did had some peace, kaze Brer

Fox done got skittish 'bout puttin' de clamps on Brer Rabbit.

"One day, w'en Brer Rabbit, en Brer Fox, en Brer Coon, en Brer B'ar, en a whole lot un um wuz clearin' up a new groun' fer ter plant a roas'n'year patch, de sun 'gun ter git sorter hot, en Brer Rabbit he got tired; but he didn't let on, kaze he 'fear'd de balance un um'd call 'im lazy, en he keep on totin' off trash en pilin' up bresh, twel bimeby he holler out dat he gotter brier in his han', en den he take'n slip off, en

hunt fer cool place fer ter res'. Atter w'ile he come 'crosst a well wid a bucket hangin' in it.

"'Dat look cool,' sez Brer Rabbit, sezee, 'en cool I speck she is. I'll des 'bout git in dar en take a nap,' en wid dat in he jump, he did, en he ain't no sooner fix hisse'f dan de bucket 'gun ter go down.'"

"Wasn't the Rabbit scared, Uncle Remus?" asked the little boy.

"Honey, dey ain't been no wusser skeer'd beas' sence de worril begin dan dish yer same Brer Rabbit. He fa'rly had a ager. He know whar he cum fum, but he dunner whar he gwine. Dreckly he feel de bucket hit de water, en dar she sot, but Brer Rabbit he keep mighty still, kaze he dunner w'at minnit gwineter be de nex'. He des lay dar en shuck en shiver.

"Brer Fox allers got one eye on Brer Rabbit, en w'en he slip off fum de new groun', Brer Fox he sneak atter 'im. He know Brer Rabbit wuz atter some projick er nudder, en he tuck'n crope off, he did, en watch 'im. Brer Fox see Brer Rabbit come to de well en stop, en den he see 'im jump in de bucket, en den, lo en beholes, he see 'im go down outer sight. Brer Fox wuz de mos' 'stonish Fox dat you ever laid eyes on. He sot off dar in de bushes en study en study, but he don't make no head ner tails ter dis kinder bizness. Den he say ter hisse'f, sezee:

"'Well, ef dis don't bang my times,' sezee, 'den Joe's dead en Sal's a widder. Right down dar in dat well Brer Rabbit keep his money hid, en ef 'tain't dat den he done gone en 'skiver'd a gole-mine, en ef 'tain't dat, den I'm a gwineter see w'at's in dar,' sezee.

"Brer Fox crope up little nigher, he did, en lissen, but he don't year no fuss, en he keep on gittin' nigher, en yit he don't year nuthin'. Bimeby he git up close en peep down, but he don't see nuthin' en he don't year nuthin'. All dis time Brer Rabbit mighty nigh skeer'd outen his skin, en he fear'd fer ter move kaze de bucket might keel over en spill him out in de water. W'ile he sayin' his pra'rs over like a train er kyars runnin', ole Brer Fox holler out:

"'Heyo, Brer Rabbit! Who you wizzitin' down dar?' sezee.

"'Who? Me? Oh, I'm des a fishin', Brer Fox,' sez Brer Rabbit, sezee. 'I des say ter myse'f dat I'd sorter sprize you all wid a mess er fishes fer dinner, en so here I is, en dar's de fishes. I'm a fishin' fer suckers, Brer Fox,' sez Brer Rabbit, sezee.

"'Is dey many un um down dar, Brer Rabbit?' sez Brer Fox, sezee.

"'Lots un um, Brer Fox; scoze en scoze un um. De water is natally live wid um. Come down en he'p me haul um in, Brer Fox,' sez Brer Rabbit, sezee.

"'How I gwinter git down, Brer Rabbit?'

"'Jump inter de bucket, Brer Fox. Hit'll fetch you down all safe en soun'.'

"Brer Rabbit talk so happy en talk so sweet dat Brer Fox he jump in de bucket, he did, en, ez he went down, co'se his weight pull Brer Rabbit up.

W'en dey pass one nudder on de half-way groun',
Brer Rabbit he sing out:

> " 'Good-by, Brer Fox, take keer yo' cloze,
> Fer dis-is de way de worril goes;
> Some goes up en some goes down,
> You'll git ter de bottom all safe en soun'.' *

"W'en Brer Rabbit got out, he gallop off en tole
de fokes w'at de
well b'long ter dat
Brer Fox wuz down
in dar muddyin' up
de drinkin' water, en
den he gallop back
ter de well, en holler
down ter Brer Fox:

> " 'Yer come a man wid
> a great big gun—
> W'en he haul you up,
> you jump en run.' "

"What then,
Uncle Remus?"
asked the little boy,
as the old man
paused.

---

* As a Northern friend suggests that this story may be somewhat obscure, it may be as well to state that the well is supposed
to be supplied with a rope over a wheel, or pulley, with a bucket
at each end.

In des 'bout half n'our, honey, bofe un um wuz
back in de new groun' wukkin des like dey never
heer'd er no well, ceppin' dat eve'y now'n den Brer
Rabbit'd bust out in er laff, en old Brer Fox, he'd git
a spell er de dry grins."

XVII

MR. RABBIT NIBBLES UP THE BUTTER

"DE animils en de creeturs," said Uncle Remus,
shaking his coffee around in the bottom of his tin-
cup, in order to gather up all the sugar, "dey kep' on
gittin' mo' en mo' familious wid wunner nudder, twel
bimeby, 'twan't long 'fo' Brer Rabbit, en Brer Fox, en
Brer Possum got ter sorter bunchin' der perwishuns
tergedder in de same shanty. Atter w'ile de roof
sorter 'gun ter leak, en one day Brer Rabbit, en Brer
Fox, en Brer Possum, 'semble fer ter see ef dey can't
kinder patch her up. Dey had a big day's work in
front un um, en dey fotch der dinner wid um. Dey
lump de vittles up in one pile, en de butter w'at Brer
Fox brung, dey goes en puts in de spring-'ouse fer ter
keep cool, en den dey went ter wuk, en 'twan't long
'fo' Brer Rabbit stummuck 'gun ter sorter growl en
pester 'im. Dat butter er Brer Fox sot heavy on his
mine, en his mouf water eve'y time he 'member 'bout
it. Present'y he say ter hisse'f dat he bleedzd ter have

a nip at dat butter, en den he lay his plans, he did.
Fus' news you know, w'ile dey wuz all wukkin' 'long,
Brer Rabbit raise his head quick en fling his years
forrerd en holler out:

"'Here I is. W'at you want wid me?' en off he
put like sump'n wuz atter 'im.

"He sallied 'roun', ole Brer Rabbit did, en atter
he make sho dat nobody ain't foller'n un 'im, inter de

spring-'ouse he bounces,
en dar he stays twel he
git a bait er butter. Den
he santer on back en go
to wuk.

"'Whar you bin?' sez
Brer Fox, sezee.

"'I hear my chilluns
callin' me,' sez Brer Rabbit, sezee, 'en I hatter go
see w'at dey want. My
ole 'oman done gone en
tuck mighty sick,' sezee.

"Dey wuk on twel
bimeby de butter tas'e so
good dat ole Brer Rabbit want some mo'. Den he raise
up his head, he did, en holler out:

"'Heyo! Hole on! I'm a comin'!' en off he put.

"Dis time he stay right smart w'ile, en w'en he git
back Brer Fox ax him whar he bin.

"'I been ter see my ole 'oman, en she's a sinkin',' sezee.

"Dreckly Brer Rabbit hear um callin' 'im ag'in en off he goes, en dis time, bless yo' soul, he gits de butter out so clean dat he kin see hisse'f in de bottom er de bucket. He scrape it clean en lick it dry, en den he go back ter wuk lookin' mo' samer dan a nigger w'at de patter-rollers bin had holt un.

"'How's yo' ole 'oman dis time?' sez Brer Fox, sezee.

"'I'm oblije ter you, Brer Fox,' sez Brer Rabbit, sezee, 'but I'm fear'd she's done gone by now,' en dat sorter make Brer Fox en Brer Possum feel in moanin' wid Brer Rabbit.

"Bimeby, w'en dinner-time come, dey all got out der vittles, but Brer Rabbit keep on lookin' lonesome, en Brer Fox en Brer Possum dey sorter rustle roun' fer ter see ef dey can't make Brer Rabbit feel sorter splimmy."

"What is that, Uncle Remus?" asked the little boy.

"Sorter splimmy-splammy, honey—sorter like he in a crowd—sorter like his ole 'oman ain't dead ez she mout be. You know how fokes duz w'en dey gits whar people's a moanin'."

The little boy didn't know, fortunately for him, and Uncle Remus went on:

"Brer Fox en Brer Possum rustle roun', dey did, gittin out de vittles, en bimeby Brer Fox, he say, sezee:

" 'Brer Possum, you run down ter de spring en fetch de butter, en I'll sail 'roun' yer en set de table,' sezee.

"Brer Possum, he lope off atter de butter, en dreckly here he come lopin' back wid his years a trimblin' en his tongue a hangin' out. Brer Fox, he holler out:

" 'W'at de matter now, Brer Possum?' sezee.

" 'You all better run yer, fokes,' sez Brer Possum, sezee. 'De las' drap er dat butter done gone!'

" 'Whar she gone?' sez Brer Fox, sezee.

" 'Look like she dry up,' sez Brer Possum, sezee.

"Den Brer Rabbit, he look sorter sollum, he did, en he up'n say, sezee.

" 'I speck dat butter melt in somebody mouf,' sezee.

"Den dey went down ter de spring wid Brer Possum, en sho nuff de butter done gone. W'iles dey wuz sputin' over de wunderment, Brer Rabbit say he see tracks all 'roun' dar, en he p'int out dat ef dey'll all go ter sleep, he kin ketch de chap w'at stole de butter. Den dey all lie down en Brer Fox en Brer Possum dey soon drapt off ter sleep, but Brer Rabbit he stay 'wake, en w'en de time come he raise up easy en smear Brer Possum mouf wid de butter on his paws, en den he run off en nibble up de bes' er de dinner w'at dey lef' layin' out, en den he come back en wake up Brer Fox, en show 'im de butter on Brer Possum mouf. Den dey wake up Brer Possum, en tell 'im

'bout it, but c'ose Brer Possum 'ny it ter de las'. Brer
Fox, dough, he's a kinder lawyer, en he argafy dis
way—dat Brer Possum wuz de fus one at de butter,

en de fus one fer ter miss it, en mo'n dat. dar hang de
signs on his mouf. Brer Possum see dat dey got 'im
jammed up in a cornder, en den he up en say dat de
way fer ter ketch de man w'at stole de butter is ter
b'il' a big bresh-heap en set her afier, en all han's try
ter jump over, en de one w'at fall in, den he de chap
w'at stole de butter. Brer Rabbit en Brer Fox dey

bofe 'gree, dey did, en dey whirl in en b'il' de bresh-
heap, en dey b'il' her high en dey b'il' her wide, en
den dey totch her off. W'en she got ter blazin' up
good, Brer Rabbit, he tuck de fus turn. He sorter
step back, en look 'roun' en giggle, en over he went
mo' samer dan a bird flyin'. Den come Brer Fox. He
got back little fudder, en spit on his han's, en lit out
en made de jump, en he come so nigh gittin' in dat
de een' er his tail kotch afier. Ain't you never see no

fox, honey?" inquired Uncle Remus, in a tone that
implied both conciliation and information.

The little boy thought probably he had, but he wouldn't commit himself.

"Well, den," continued the old man, "nex' time you see one un um, you look right close en see ef de een' er his tail ain't w'ite. Hit's des like I tell you. Dey b'ars de skyar er dat bresh-heap down ter dis day. Dey er marked—dat's w'at dey is—dey er marked."

"And what about Brother Possum?" asked the little boy.

"Ole Brer Possum, he tuck a runnin' start, he did, en he come lumberin' 'long, en he lit—kerblam!— right in de middle er de fier, en dat wuz de las' er ole Brer Possum."

"But, Uncle Remus, Brother Possum didn't steal the butter after all," said the little boy, who was not at all satisfied with such summary injustice.

"Dat w'at make I say w'at I duz, honey. In dis worril, lots er fokes is gotter suffer fer udder fokes sins. Look like hit's mighty onwrong; but hit's des dat away. Tribbalashun seem like she's a waitin' roun' de cornder fer ter ketch one en all un us, honey."

XVIII

MR. RABBIT FINDS HIS MATCH AT LAST

"Hɪт look like ter me dat I let on de udder night dat in dem days w'en de creeturs wuz santer'n 'roun' same like fokes, none un um wuz brash nuff fer ter ketch up wid Brer Rabbit," remarked Uncle Remus, reflectively.

"Yes," replied the little boy, "that's what you said."

"Well, den," continued the old man with unction, "dar's whar my 'membunce gin out, kaze Brer Rabbit did git kotched up wid, en hit cool 'im off like po'in' spring water on one er deze yer biggity fices."

"How was that, Uncle Remus?" asked the little boy.

"One day w'en Brer Rabbit wuz gwine lippity-clippitin' down de road, he meet up wid ole Brer Tarrypin, en atter dey pass de time er day wid wun-

ner nudder, Brer Rabbit, he 'low dat he wuz much 'blije ter Brer Tarrypin fer de han' he tuck in de rumpus dat day down at Miss Meadows's."

"When he dropped off of the water-shelf on the Fox's head," suggested the little boy.

"Dat's de same time, honey. Den Brer Tarrypin

'low dat Brer Fox run mighty fas' dat day, but dat ef
he'd er bin atter 'im stidder Brer Rabbit, he'd er
kotch 'im. Brer Rabbit say he could er kotch 'im
hisse'f but he didn't keer 'bout leavin' de ladies. Dey
keep on talkin', dey did, twel bimeby dey gotter 'sputin' 'bout w'ich wuz de swif'es'. Brer Rabbit, he say
he kin outrun Brer Tarrypin, en Brer Tarrypin, he
des vow dat he kin outrun Brer Rabbit. Up en down
dey had it, twel fus news you know Brer Tarrypin say
he got a fifty-dollar bill in de chink er de chimbly at
home, en dat bill done tole 'im dat he could beat Brer
Rabbit in a fa'r race. Den Brer Rabbit say he got a
fifty-dollar bill w'at say dat he kin leave Brer Tarrypin so fur behime, dat he could sow barley ez he
went 'long en hit 'ud be ripe nuff fer ter cut by de
time Brer Tarrypin pass dat way.

"Enny how dey make de bet en put up de money,
en old Brer Tukky Buzzard, he wuz summonzd fer
ter be de jedge, en de stakeholder; en 'twan't long 'fo'
all de 'rangements wuz made. De race wuz a five-mile
heat, en de groun' wuz medjud off, en at de een' er
ev'ey mile a pos' wuz stuck up. Brer Rabbit wuz ter
run down de big road, en Brer Tarrypin, he say he'd
gallup thoo de woods. Fokes tole 'im he could git
long faster in de road, but ole Brer Tarrypin, he know
w'at he doin'. Miss Meadows en de gals en mos' all de
nabers got win' er de fun, en w'en de day wuz sot dey
'termin' fer ter be on han'. Brer Rabbit he train his-

se'f ev'ey day, en he skip over de groun' des ez gayly
ez a June cricket. Ole Brer Tarrypin, he lay low in de
swamp. He had a wife en th'ee chilluns, old Brer
Tarrypin did, en dey wuz all de ve'y spit en image er
de ole man. Ennybody w'at know one fum de udder
gotter take a spy-glass, en den dey er li'ble fer ter git
fooled.

"Dat's de way marters stan' twel de day er de
race, en on dat day, ole Brer Tarrypn, en his ole
'oman, en his th'ee chilluns, dey got up 'fo' sun-up, en
went ter de place. De ole 'oman, she tuck 'er stan'
nigh de fus' mile-pos', she did, en de chilluns nigh de
udders, up ter de las', en dar old Brer Tarrypin, he
tuck his stan'. Bimeby, here come de fokes: Jedge
Buzzard, he come, en Miss Meadows en de gals, dey
come, en den yer come Brer Rabbit wid ribbons tied
'roun' his neck en streamin' fum his years. De fokes
all went ter de udder een' er de track fer ter see
how dey come out. W'en de time come Jedge Buzzard strut 'roun' en pull out his watch, en holler
out:

"'Gents, is you ready?'

"Brer Rabbit, he say 'yes,' en old Miss Tarrypin
holler 'go' fum de aidge er de woods. Brer Rabbit,
he lit out on de race, en old Miss Tarrypin, she put
out for home. Jedge Buzzard, he riz en skimmed 'long
fer ter see dat de race wuz runned fa'r. W'en Brer
Rabbit got ter de fus' mile-pos' wunner de Tarrypin

chilluns crawl out de woods, he did, en make fer de
place. Brer Rabbit, he holler out:

" 'Whar is
you, Brer Tar-
rypin?'

" 'Yer I come
a bulgin',' sez
de   Tarrypin,
sezee.

"Brer Rabbit
so glad he's
ahead dat he
put out harder
dan ever, en de

Tarrypin, he make fer home. W'en he come ter de
nex' pos', nudder Tarrypin crawl out er de woods.

" 'Whar is you, Brer Tarrypin?' sez Brer Rabbit,
sezee.

" 'Yer I come a bilin',' sez de Tarrypin, sezee.

"Brer Rabbit, he lit out, he did, en come ter nex'
pos', en dar wuz de Tarrypin. Den he come ter nex',
en dar wuz de Tarrypin. Den he had one mo' mile
fer ter run, en he feel like he gittin' bellust. Bimeby,
ole Brer Tarrypin look way off down de road en he
see Jedge Buzzard sailin' 'long en he know hit's time
fer 'im fer ter be up. So he scramble outen de woods,
en roll 'cross de ditch, en shuffle thoo de crowd er
folks en git ter de mile-pos' en crawl behime it.

Bimeby, fus' news you know, yer come Brer Rabbit. He look 'roun' en he don't see Brer Tarrypin, en den he squall out:

"'Gimme de money, Brer Buzzard, Gimme de money!'

"Den Miss Meadows en de gals, dey holler and laff fit ter kill deyse'f, en ole Brer Tarrypin, he raise up fum behime de pos' en sez, sezee:

"Ef you'll gimme time fer ter ketch my breff, gents en ladies, one en all, I speck I'll finger dat money myse'f,' sezee, en sho nuff, Brer Tarrypin tie de pu's 'roun' his neck en skaddle * off home."

"But, Uncle Remus," said the little boy, dolefully, "that was cheating."

"Co'se, honey. De creeturs 'gun ter cheat, en den fokes tuck it up, en hit keep on spreadin'. Hit mighty

---

* It may be interesting to note here that in all probability the word "skedaddle," about which there was some controversy during the war, came from the Virginia negro's use of "skaddle," which is a corruption of "scatter." The matter, however, is hardly worth referring to.

ketchin', en you mine yo' eye, honey, dat somebody
don't cheat you 'fo' yo' ha'r git gray ez de ole nigger's."

XIX

THE FATE OF MR. JACK SPARROW

"You'll tromple on dat bark twel hit won't be
fitten fer ter fling 'way, let 'lone make hoss-collars
out'n," said Uncle Remus, as the little boy came running into his cabin out of the rain. All over the floor
long strips of "wahoo" bark were spread, and these
the old man was weaving into horse-collars.

"I'll sit down, Uncle Remus," said the little boy.

"Well, den, you better, honey," responded the old
man, "kaze I 'spizes fer ter have my wahoo trompled
on. Ef 'twuz shucks, now, hit mout be diffunt, but I'm
a gittin' too ole fer ter be projickin' longer shuck
collars."

For a few minutes the old man went on with his
work, but with a solemn air altogether unusual. Once
or twice he sighed deeply, and the sighs ended in a
prolonged groan, that seemed to the little boy to be
the result of the most unspeakable mental agony. He
knew by experience that he had done something
which failed to meet the approval of Uncle Remus,
and he tried to remember what it was, so as to frame
an excuse; but his memory failed him. He could think
of nothing he had done calculated to stir Uncle

Remus's grief. He was not exactly seized with re-
morse, but he was very uneasy. Presently Uncle
Remus looked at him in a sad and hopeless way, and
asked:

"W'at dat long rigmarole you bin tellin' Miss Sally
'bout yo' little brer dis mawnin?"

"Which, Uncle Remus?" asked the little boy,
blushing guiltily.

"Dat des w'at I'm a axin' un you now. I hear Miss
Sally say she's a gwineter stripe his jacket, en den I
knowed you bin tellin' on 'im."

"Well, Uncle Remus, he was pulling up your
onions, and then he went and flung a rock at me,"
said the child, plaintively.

"Lemme tell you dis," said the old man, laying
down the section of horse-collar he had been plaiting,
and looking hard at the little boy—"lemme tell you
dis—der ain't no way fer ter make tattlers en tail-
b'arers turn out good. No, dey ain't. I bin mixin'
up wid fokes now gwine on eighty year, en I ain't
seed no tattler come ter no good een'. Dat I ain't.
En ef ole man M'thoozlum wuz livin' clean twel yit,
he'd up'n tell you de same. Sho ez youer settin' dar.
You 'member w'at 'come er de bird w'at went tattlin'
'roun' 'bout Brer Rabbit?"

The little boy didn't remember, but he was very
anxious to know, and he also wanted to know what
kind of a bird it was that so disgraced itself.

"Hit wuz wun-
ner dese yer uppity
little Jack Sparrers,
I speck," said the
old man; "dey wuz
allers bodder'n'
longer udder
fokes's bizness, en
dey keeps at it
down ter dis day—
peckin' yer, en
pickin' dar, en
scratchin' out yan-
der. One day, atter
he bin fool by ole
Brer Tarrypin, Brer
Rabbit wuz settin'
down in de woods
studdyin' how he
wuz gwineter git
even. He feel
mighty lonesome,
en he feel mighty
mad, Brer Rabbit

95

did. Tain't put down in de tale, but I speck he cusst
en r'ar'd 'roun' considerbul. Leas'ways, he wuz settin'
out dar by hisse'f, en dar he sot, en study en study,
twel bimeby he jump up en holler out:

"'Well, dog-gone my cats ef I can't gallop 'roun'
ole Brer Fox, en I'm gwineter do it. I'll show Miss
Meadows en de gals dat I'm de boss er Brer Fox,'
sezee.

"Jack Sparrer up in de tree, he hear Brer Rabbit,
he did, en he sing out:

"'I'm gwine tell Brer Fox! I'm gwine tell Brer Fox!
Chick-a-biddy-win'-a-blowin'-acuns-fallin'! I'm gwine
tell Brer Fox!'"

Uncle Remus accompanied the speech of the bird
with a peculiar whistling sound in his throat, that was
a marvelous imitation of a sparrow's chirp, and the
little boy clapped his hands with delight, and insisted
on a repetition.

"Dis kinder tarrify Brer Rabbit, en he skasely know
w'at he gwine do; but bimeby he study ter hisse'f dat
de man w'at see Brer Fox fus wuz boun' ter have de
inturn, en den he go hoppin' off to'rds home. He
didn't got fur w'en who should he meet but Brer Fox,
en den Brer Rabbit, he open up:

"'W'at dis twix' you en me, Brer Fox?' sez Brer
Rabbit, sezee. 'I hear tell you gwine ter sen' me ter
'struckshun, en nab my fambly, en 'stroy my shanty,'
sezee.

"'Den Brer Fox he git mighty mad.

"'Who bin tellin' you all dis?' sezee.

"Brer Rabbit make like he didn't want ter tell, but Brer Fox he 'sist en 'sist, twel at las' Brer Rabbit he up en tell Brer Fox dat he hear Jack Sparrer say all dis.

"'Co'se,' sez Brer Rabbit, sezee, 'w'en Brer Jack Sparrer tell me dat I flew up, I did, en I use some langwidge w'ich I'm mighty glad dey weren't no ladies 'round' nowhars so dey could hear me go on,' sezee.

"Brer Fox he sorter gap, he did, en say he speck he better be sa'nter'n on. But, bless yo' soul, honey, Brer Fox ain't sa'nter fur, 'fo' Jack Sparrer flipp down on a 'simmon-bush by de side er de road, en holler out:

"'Brer Fox! Oh, Brer Fox!—Brer Fox!'

"Brer Fox he des sorter can-ter 'long, he did, en make like he don't hear 'im. Den Jack Sparrer up'n sing out agin:

"'Brer Fox! Oh, Brer Fox!

Hole on, Brer Fox! I got some news fer you. Wait Brer Fox! Hit'll 'stonish you.'

"Brer Fox he make like he don't see Jack Sparrer, ner needer do he hear 'im, but bimeby he lay down by de road, en sorter stretch hisse'f like he fixin' fer ter nap. De tattlin' Jack Sparrer he flew'd 'long, en keep on callin' Brer Fox, but Brer Fox, he ain't sayin' nuthin'. Den little Jack Sparrer, he hop down on de groun' en flutter 'roun' 'mongst de trash. Dis sorter 'track Brer Fox 'tenshun, en he look at de tattlin' bird, en de bird he keep on callin':

" 'I got sump'n fer ter tell you, Brer Fox.'

" 'Git on my tail, little Jack Sparrer,' sez Brer Fox, sezee, 'kaze I'm de'f in one year, en I can't hear out'n de udder. Git on my tail,' sezee.

"Den de little bird he up'n hop on Brer Fox's tail.

" 'Git on my back, little Jack Sparrer, kaze I'm de'f in one year en I can't hear out'n de udder.'

"Den de little bird hop on his back.

" 'Hop on my head, little Jack Sparrer, kaze I'm de'f in bofe years.'

"Up hop de little bird.

" 'Hop on my toof, little Jack Sparrer, kaze I'm de'f in one year en I can't hear out'n de udder.'

"De tattlin' little bird hop on Brer Fox's toof, en den—"

Here Uncle Remus paused, opened wide his mouth

and closed it again in a way that told the whole story.*

"Did the Fox eat the bird all—all—up?" asked the little boy.

"Jedge B'ar come 'long nex' day," replied Uncle Remus, "en he fine some fedders, en fum dat word went roun' dat ole man Squinch Owl done kotch nudder watzizname."

XX

HOW MR. RABBIT SAVED HIS MEAT

"ONE time," said Uncle Remus, whetting his knife slowly and thoughtfully on the palm of his hand, and gazing reflectively in the fire—"one time Brer Wolf—"

"Why, Uncle Remus!" the little boy broke in, "I thought you said the Rabbit scalded the Wolf to death a long time ago."

The old man was fairly caught and he knew it; but this made little difference to him. A frown gath-

---

* An Atlanta friend heard this story in Florida, but an alligator was substituted for the fox, and a little boy for the rabbit. There is another version in which the impertinent gosling goes to tell the fox something her mother has said, and is caught; and there may be other versions. I have adhered to the middle Georgia version, which is characteristic enough. It may be well to state that there are different versions of all the stories—the shrewd narrators of the mythology of the old plantation adapting themselves with ready tact to the years, tastes, and expectations of their juvenile audiences.

ered on his usually serene brow as he turned his gaze
upon the child—a frown in which both scorn and indignation were visible. Then all at once he seemed
to regain control of himself. The frown was chased
away by a look of Christian resignation.

"Dar now! W'at I tell you?" he exclaimed as if addressing a witness concealed under the bed. "Ain't
I done tole you so? Bless grashus! ef chilluns ain't
gittin' so dey knows mo'n ole fokes, en dey'll spute
longer you en spute longer you, ceppin der ma call
um, w'ich I speck twon't be long 'fo' she will, en den
I'll set yere by de chimbly-cornder en git some peace
er mine. W'en ole Miss wuz livin'," continued the old
man, still addressing some imaginary person, "hit 'uz
mo'n enny her chilluns 'ud dast ter do ter come
'sputin' longer me, en Mars John'll tell you de same
enny day you ax 'im."

"Well, Uncle Remus, you know you said the Rabbit poured hot water on the Wolf and killed him,"
said the little boy.

The old man pretended not to hear. He was engaged in searching among some scraps of leather
under his chair, and kept on talking to the imaginary
person. Finally, he found and drew forth a nicely
plaited whip-thong with a red snapper all waxed and
knotted.

"I wuz fixin' up a wi'p fer a little chap," he continued, with a sigh, "but, bless grashus! 'fo' I kin git

'er done, de little chap done grow'd up twel he know mo'n I duz."

The child's eyes filled with tears and his lips began to quiver, but he said nothing; whereupon Uncle Remus immediately melted.

"I 'clar' to goodness," he said, reaching out and taking the little boy tenderly by the hand, "ef you ain't de ve'y spit en image er ole Miss w'en I brung 'er de las' news er de war. Hit's des like skeerin' up a ghos' w'at you ain't fear'd un."

Then there was a pause, the old man patting the little child's hand caressingly.

"You ain't mad, is you, honey?" Uncle Remus asked finally, "kaze ef you is, I'm gwine out yere en butt my head 'gin de do' jam'."

But the little boy wasn't mad. Uncle Remus had conquered him and he had conquered Uncle Remus in pretty much the same way before. But it was some time before Uncle Remus would go on with the story. He had to be coaxed. At last, however, he settled himself back in the chair and began:

"Co'se, honey, hit mout er bin ole Brer Wolf, er hit mout er bin er n'er Brer Wolf; it mout er bin 'fo' he got kotch up wid, er it mout er bin atterwards. Ez de tale wer gun to me des dat away I gin it unter you. One time Brer Wolf wuz comin' 'long home fum a fishin' frolic. He s'anter 'long de road, he did, wid his string er fish 'cross his shoulder, wen fus news

you know ole Miss Pa'tridge, she hop outer de bushes
en flutter 'long right at Brer Wolf nose. Brer Wolf
he say ter hisse'f dat ole Miss Pa'tridge tryin' fer ter
toll 'im 'way fum her nes', en wid dat he lay his fish
down en put out inter de bushes whar ole Miss
Pa'tridge come fum, en 'bout dat time Brer Rabbit,
he happen 'long. Dar wuz de fishes, en dar wuz
Brer Rabbit, en w'en dat de case w'at you speck
a sorter innerpen'ent man like Brer Rabbit gwine do?
I kin tell you dis, dat dem fishes ain't stay whar
Brer Wolf put um at, en w'en Brer Wolf come
back dey wuz gone.

"Brer Wolf, he sot
down en scratch his
head, he did, en
study en study, en
den hit sorter rush
inter his mine dat
Brer Rabbit bin 'long
dar, en den Brer
Wolf, he put out fer
Brer Rabbit house,
en w'en he git dar he
hail 'im. Brer Rabbit,
he dunno nuthin' tall
'bout no fishes. Brer
Wolf he up'n say he
bleedzd ter b'leeve

Brer Rabbit got dem fishes. Brer Rabbit 'ny it up
en down, but Brer Wolf stan' to it dat Brer Rabbit
got dem fishes. Brer Rabbit, he say dat if Brer Wolf
b'leeve he go de fishes, den he give Brer Wolf lief
fer ter kill de bes' cow he got. Brer Wolf, he tuck
Brer Rabbit at his word, en go off ter de pastur' en
drive up de cattle en kill Brer Rabbit bes' cow.

"Brer Rabbit, he hate mighty bad fer ter lose his
cow, but he lay nis plans, en he tell his chilluns dat
he gwineter have dat beef yit. Brer Wolf, he bin tuck
up by de patter-rollers 'fo' now, en he mighty skeerd
un um, en fus news you know, yer come Brer Rabbit
hollerin' en tellin' Brer Wolf dat de patter-rollers
comin'.

"'You run en hide, Brer Wolf,' sez Brer Rabbit,
sezee, 'en I'll stay yer en take keer er de cow twel
you gits back,' sezee.

"Soon's Brer Wolf hear talk er de patter-rollers,
he scramble off inter de underbrush like he bin shot
out'n a gun. En he want mo'n gone 'fo' Brer Rabbit,
he whirl in en skunt de cow en salt de hide down, en
den he tuck'n cut up de kyarkiss en stow it 'way in
de smoke-'ouse, en den he tuck'n stick de een' er de
cow-tail in de groun'. Atter he gone en done all dis,
den Brer Rabbit he squall out fer Brer Wolf:

"'Run yer, Brer Wolf! Run yer! Yo' cow gwine in
de groun'! Run yer!'

"W'en ole Brer Wolf got dar, w'ich he come er scootin', dar wuz Brer Rabbit hol'in' n ter de cow-tail, fer ter keep it fum gwine in de groun'. Brer Wolf, he kotch holt, en dey 'gin a pull er two en up come de tail. Den Brer Rabbit, he wink his off eye en say, sezee:

" 'Dar! de tail done pull out en de cow gone,' sezee.

"But Brer Wolf he wer'n't de man fer ter give it up dat away, en he got 'im a spade, n a pick-axe, en a shovel, en he dig en dig fer dat cow twel diggin' wuz pas' all endu'unce, en ole Brer Rabbit he sot up dar in his front po'ch en smoke his seegyar. Eve'y time ole Brer Wolf stuck de pick-axe in de clay, Brer Rabbit, he giggle ter his chilluns:

" 'He diggy, diggy, diggy, but no meat dar! He diggy, diggy, diggy, but no meat dar!'

"Kase all de time de cow wuz layin' pile up in his smoke-'ouse, en him en his chilluns wuz eatin' fried beef an inguns eve'y time dey mouf water.

"Now den, honey, you take dis yer w'ip," continued the old man, twining the leather thong around the little boy's neck, "en scamper up ter de big 'ouse en tell Miss Sally fer ter gin you some un it de nex' time she fine yo' tracks in de sugar-bairl."

XXI

MR. RABBIT MEETS HIS MATCH AGAIN

"Dere wuz nudder man dat sorter play it sharp on Brer Rabbit," said Uncle Remus, as, by some mysterious process, he twisted a hog's bristle into the end of a piece of thread—an operation which the little boy watched with great interest. "In dem days," continued the old man, "de creeturs kyar'd on marters same ez fokes. Dey went inter fahmin', en I speck ef de troof wuz ter come out, dey kep' sto', en had der camp-meetin' times en der bobbycues' w'en de wedder wuz 'greeble."

Uncle Remus evidently thought that the little boy wouldn't like to hear of any further discomfiture of Brer Rabbit, who had come to be a sort of hero, and he was not mistaken.

"I thought the Terrapin was the only one that fooled the Rabbit," said the little boy, dismally.

"Hit's des like I tell you, honey. Dey ain't no smart man, 'cep' w'at dey's a smarter. Ef ole Brer Rabbit hadn't er got kotch up wid, de nabers 'ud er took 'im for a h'ant, en in dem times dey bu'nt witches 'fo' you could squinch yo' eyeballs. Dey did dat."

"Who fooled the Rabbit this time?" the little boy asked.

When Uncle Remus had the bristle "sot" in the thread, he proceeded with the story:

"One time Brer Rabbit en ole Brer Buzzard 'cluded dey'd sorter go snacks, en crap tergedder. Hit wuz a

mighty good year, en de truck tu'n out monstus well, but bimeby, w'en de time come fer dividjun, hit come ter light dat ole Brer Buzzard ain't got nuthin'. De crap wuz all gone, en dey want nuthin' dar fer ter show fer it. Brer Rabbit, he make like he in a wuss fix'n Brer Buzzard, en he mope 'roun', he did, like he fear'd dey gwineter sell 'im out.

"Brer Buzzard, he ain't sayin' nuthin', but he keep up a monstus thinkin', en one day he come 'long en

holler en tell Brer Rabbit dat he done fine rich gole-
mine des 'cross de river.

"'You come en go 'longer me, Brer Rabbit,' sez
Brer Tukky Buzzard, sezee. 'I'll scratch en you kin
grabble, en 'tween de two un us we'll make short
wuk er dat gole-mine,' sezee.

"Brer Rabbit, he wuz high up fer de job, but he
study en study, he did, how he gwinter git 'cross de
water, kaze ev'y time he git his foot wet all de fambly
kotch cole. Den he up'n ax Brer Buzzard how he
gwine do, en Brer Buzzard he up'n say dat he kyar
Brer Rabbit 'cross, en wid dat ole Brer Buzzard, he
squot down, he did, en spread his wings, en Brer
Rabbit, he mounted, en up dey riz." There was a
pause.

"What did the Buzzard do then?" asked the little
boy.

"Dey riz," continued Uncle Remus, "en w'en dey
lit, dey lit in de top er de highest sorter pine, en de
pine w'at dey lit in wuz growin' on er ilun, en de ilun
wuz in de middle er de river, wid de deep water
runnin' all 'roun'. Dey ain't mo'n lit 'fo' Brer Rabbit,
he know w'ich way de win' 'uz blowin', en by de time
ole Brer Buzzard got hisse'f ballunce on a lim', Brer
Rabbit, he up'n say, sezee:

"'Wiles we er res'n here, Brer Buzzard, en bein's
you bin so good, I got sump'n fer ter tell you,' sezee.
'I got a gole-mine er my own, one w'at I make my-

se'f, en I speck we better go back ter mine 'fo' we bodder 'longer yone,' sezee.

"Den ole Brer Buzzard, he laff, he did, twel he shake, en Brer Rabbit, he sing out:

"Hole on, Brer Buzzard! Don't flop yo' wings w'en you laff, kaze den if you duz, sump'n 'ill drap fum up yer, en my gole-mine won't do you no good, en needer will yone do me no good.'

"But 'fo' dey got down fum dar, Brer Rabbit done tole all 'bout de crap, en he hatter promus fer ter 'vide fa'r en squar. So Brer Buzzard, he kyar 'im back, en Brer Rabbit he walk weak in de knees a mont' atterwuds."

XXII

A STORY ABOUT THE LITTLE RABBITS

"FINE um whar you will en w'en you may," remarked Uncle Remus with emphasis, "good chilluns allers gits tuck keer on. Dar wuz Brer Rabbit's chilluns; dey minded der daddy en mammy fum day's een'

ter day's een'. W'en ole man Rabbit say 'scoot,' dey
scooted, en w'en ole Miss Rabbit say 'scat,' dey
scatted. Dey did dat. En dey kep der cloze clean,
en dey ain't had no smut on der nose nudder."

Involuntarily the hand of the little boy went up to
his face, and he scrubbed the end of his nose with his
coat-sleeve.

"Dey wuz good chilluns," continued the old man,
heartily, "en ef dey hadn't er bin, der wuz one time
w'en dey wouldn't er bin no little rabbits—na'er one.
Dat's w'at."

"What time was that, Uncle Remus?" the little boy
asked.

"De time w'en Brer Fox drapt in at Brer Rabbit
house, en didn't foun' nobody dar ceppin' de little
Rabbits. Ole Brer Rabbit, he wuz off some'rs raiding
on a collard patch, en ole Miss Rabbit she wuz tendin'
on a quiltin' in de naberhood, en wiles de little Rabbits wuz playin' hidin'-switch, in drapt Brer Fox.
De little Rabbits wuz so fat dat dey fa'rly make his
mouf water, but he 'member 'bout Brer Wolf, en he
skeered fer ter gobble um up ceppin' he got some
skuse. De little Rabbits, dey mighty skittish, en dey
sorter huddle deyse'f up tergedder en watch Brer
Fox motions. Brer Fox, he sot dar en study w'at
sorter skuse he gwineter make up. Bimeby he see a
great big stalk er sugar-cane stan'in' up in de cornder,
en he cle'r up his th'oat en talk biggity:

" 'Yer! you young Rabs dar, sail 'roun' yer en broke me a piece er dat sweetnin'-tree,' sezee, en den he koff.

"De little Rabbits, dey got out de sugar-cane, dey did, en dey rastle wid it, en sweat over it, but twan't no use. Dey couldn't broke it. Brer Fox, he make like he ain't watchin', but he keep on holler'n:

" 'Hurry up dar, Rabs! I'm a waitin' on you.'

"En de little Rabbits, dey hustle 'roun' en rastle wid it, but they couldn't broke it. Bimeby dey hear little bird singin' on top er de house, en de song w'at de little bird sing wuz dish yer:

" 'Take yo' toofies en gnyaw it,
Take yo' toofies en saw it,
Saw it en yoke it,
En den you kin broke it.'

"Den de little Rabbits, dey git mighty glad, en dey gnyawed de cane mos' 'fo' 'ole Brer Fox could git his legs oncrosst, en w'en dey kyard 'im de cane, Brer Fox, he sot dar en study how he gwineter make some mo' skuse fer nabbin' un um, en bimeby he git up en git down de sifter w'at wuz hangin' on de wall, en holler out:

"'Come yer, Rabs! Take dish yer sifter, en run down't de spring en fetch me some fresh water.'

"De little Rabbits, dey run down't de spring, en try ter dip up de water wid de sifter, but co'se hit all run out, en hit keep on runnin' out, twell bimeby de little Rabbits sot down en 'gun ter cry. Den de little

bird settin' up in de tree he begin fer ter sing, en dish yer's de song w'at he sing:

"'Sifter hole water same ez a tray,
    Ef you fill it wid moss en dob it wid clay;
    De Fox git madder de longer you stay—
    Fill it wid moss en dob it wid clay.'

"Up dey jump, de little Rabbits did, en dey fix de sifter so 'twon't leak, en den dey kyar de water ter ole

Brer Fox. Den Brer Fox he git mighty mad, en p'int out a great big stick er wood, en tell de little Rabbits fer ter put dat on de fier. De little chaps dey got 'roun' de wood, dey did, en dey lif' at it so hard twel dey could see der own sins, but de wood ain't budge. Den dey hear de little bird singin', en dish yer's de song w'at he sing:

> "'Spit in yo' han's en tug it en toll it,
>   En git behine it, en push it, en pole it;
>   Spit in yo' han's en r'ar back en roll it.'

"En des 'bout de time dey got de wood on de fier, der daddy, he come skippin' in, en de little bird, he flew'd away. Brer Fox, he seed his game wuz up, en 'twan't long 'fo' he make his skuse en start fer ter go.

"'You better stay en take a snack wid me, Brer Fox,' sez Brer Rabbit, sezee. 'Sence Brer Wolf done quite comin' en settin' up wid me, I gittin' so I feels right lonesome dese long nights,' sezee.

"But Brer Fox, he button up his coat-collar tight en des put out fer home. En dat w'at you better do, honey, kaze I see Miss Sally's shadder sailin' backerds en for'ds 'fo' de winder, en de fus' news you know she'll be spectin' un you."

XXIII

MR. RABBIT AND MR. BEAR

"Dar wuz one season," said Uncle Remus, pulling thoughtfully at his whiskers, "w'en Brer Fox say to hisse'f dat he speck he better whirl in en plant a goober-patch, en in dem days, mon, hit wuz tech en go. De wud wern't mo'n out'n his mouf 'fo' de groun' 'uz brok'd up en de goobers 'uz planted. Ole Brer Rabbit, he sot off en watch de motions, he did, en he sorter shet one eye en sing to his chilluns:

> " 'Ti-yi! Tungalee!
> I eat um pea, I pick um pea.
> Hit grow in de groun', hit grow so free;
> Ti-yi! dem goober pea.'

"Sho' 'nuff w'en de goobers 'gun ter ripen up, eve'y time Brer Fox go down ter his patch, he fine whar somebody bin grabblin' 'mongst de vines, en he git mighty mad. He sorter speck who de somebody is, but ole Brer Rabbit he cover his tracks so cute dat Brer Fox dunner how ter ketch 'im. Bimeby, one day Brer Fox take a walk all roun' de groun'-pea patch, en 'twan't long 'fo' he fine a crack in de fence whar de rail done bin rub right smoove, en right dar he sot 'im a trap. He tuck'n ben' down a hick'ry saplin',

growin' in de fence-cornder, en tie one een' un a
plow-line on de top, en in de udder een' he fix a
loop-knot, en dat he fasten wid a trigger right in de
crack. Nex' mawnin' w'en ole Brer Rabbit come slippin' 'long en crope thoo de crack, de loop-knot kotch

'im behime de fo'legs, en de saplin' flew'd up, en dar
he wuz 'twix' de heavens en de yeth. Dar he swung,
en he fear'd he gwineter fall, en he fear'd he wer'n't
gwineter fall. W'ile he wuz a fixin' up a tale fer Brer

Fox, he hear a lumberin' down de road, en present'y yer cum ole Brer B'ar amblin' 'long fum whar he bin takin' a bee-tree. Brer Rabbit, he hail 'im:

"'Howdy, Brer B'ar!'

"Brer Ba'r, he look 'roun en bimeby he see Brer Rabbit swingin' fum de saplin', en he holler out:

"'Heyo, Brer Rabbit! How you come on dis mawnin'?'

"'Much oblije, I'm middlin', Brer B'ar,' sez Brer Rabbit, sezee.

"Den Brer B'ar, he ax Brer Rabbit w'at he doin' up dar in de elements, en Brer Rabbit, he up'n say he makin' dollar minnit. Brer B'ar, he say how. Brer Rabbit say he keepin' crows out'n Brer Fox's groun'-pea patch, en den he ax Brer B'ar ef he don't wanter make dollar minnit, kaze he got big fambly er chilluns fer to take keer un, en den he make sech nice skeercrow. Brer B'ar 'low dat he take de job, en den Brer Rabbit show 'im how ter ben' down de saplin', en 'twan't long 'fo' Brer B'ar wuz swingin' up dar in Brer Rabbit place. Den Brer Rabbit, he put out fer Brer Fox house, en w'en he got dar he sing out:

"'Brer Fox! Oh, Brer Fox! Come out yer, Brer Fox, en I'll show you de man w'at bin stealin' yo' goobers.'

"Brer Fox, he grab up his walkin'-stick, en bofe un um went runnin' back down ter der goober-patch, en w'en dey got dar, sho 'nuff, dar wuz ole Brer B'ar.

"'Oh, yes! youer kotch, is you?' sez Brer Fox, en 'fo' Brer B'ar could 'splain, Brer Rabbit he jump up en down, en holler out:

"'Hit 'im in de mouf, Brer Fox; hit 'im in de mouf'; en Brer Fox, he draw back wid de walkin'-cane, en blip he tuck 'im, en eve'y time Brer B'ar'd try ter 'splain, Brer Fox'd shower down on him.

"W'iles all dis 'uz gwine on, Brer Rabbit, he slip off en git in a mud-hole en des lef' his eyes stickin' out, kaze he know'd dat Brer B'ar'd be a comin' atter

'im. Sho 'nuff, bimeby here come Brer B'ar down de
road, en w'en he git ter de mud-hole, he say:

"'Howdy, Brer Frog; is you seed Brer Rabbit go
by yer?'

"'He des gone by,' sez Brer Rabbit, en ole man
B'ar tuck off down de road like a skeer'd mule, en
Brer Rabbit, he come out en dry hisse'f in de sun, en
go home ter his fambly same ez enny udder man."

"The Bear didn't catch the Rabbit, then?" inquired
the little boy, sleepily.

"Jump up fum dar, honey!" exclaimed Uncle
Remus, by way of reply. "I ain't got no time fer ter
be settin' yer proppin' yo' eyeleds open."

XXIV

MR. BEAR CATCHES OLD MR. BULL-FROG

"WELL, Uncle Remus," said the little boy, count-
ing to see if he hadn't lost a marble somewhere, "the
Bear didn't catch the Rabbit after all, did he?"

"Now you talkin', honey," replied the old man, his
earnest face breaking up into little eddies of smiles
—"now you talkin' sho. 'Tain't bin proned inter no
Brer B'ar fer ter kotch Brer Rabbit. Hit sorter like
settin' a mule fer ter trap a hummin'-bird. But Brer
B'ar, he tuck'n got hisse'f inter some mo' trubble,
w'ich it look like it mighty easy. Ef folks could make
der livin' longer gittin' inter trubble," continued the

old man, looking curiously at the little boy, "ole Miss
Favers wouldn't be bodder'n yo' ma fer ter borry a
cup full er sugar eve'y now en den; en it look like ter
me dat I knows
a nigger dat
wouldn't be
squattin' 'roun'
yer makin' dese
yer fish-baskits."

"How did the
Bear get into
more trouble,
Uncle Remus?"
asked the little
boy.

"Natchul,
honey. Brer B'ar,
he tuck a notion
dat ole Brer
Bull-frog wuz de
man w'at fool
'im, en he say dat he'd come up wid 'im ef 'twuz a
year atterwuds. But 'twan't no year, an 'twan't no
mont', en mo'n dat, hit wan't skasely a week, w'en
bimeby one day Brer B'ar wuz gwine home fum de
takin' un a bee-tree, en lo en beholes, who should
he see but ole Brer Bull-frog settin' out on de aidge
er de mud-muddle fas' 'sleep! Brer B'ar drap his axe,

he did, en crope up, en retch out wid his paw, en
scoop ole Brer Bull-frog in des dis away." Here the
old man used his hand ladle-fashion, by way of illus-
tration. "He scoop 'im in, en dar he wuz. W'en Brer
B'ar got his clampers on 'im good, he sot down en
talk at 'im.

"'Howdy, Brer Bull-frog, howdy! En how yo'
fambly? I hope deyer well, Brer Bull-frog, kaze dis
day you got some bizness wid me w'at'll las' you a
mighty long time.'

"Brer Bull-frog, he dunner w'at ter say. He dunner
wat's up, en he don't say nuthin'. Ole Brer B'ar he
keep runnin' on:

"'Youer de man w'at tuck en fool me 'bout Brer
Rabbit t'er day. You had yo' fun, Brer Bull-frog, en
now I'll git mine.'

"Den Brer Bull-frog, he gin ter git skeerd, he did,
en he up'n say:

"'W'at I bin doin', Brer B'ar? How I bin foolin'
you?'

"Den Brer B'ar laff, en make like he dunno, but
he keep on talkin'.

"'Oh, no, Brer Bull-frog! You ain't de man w'at
stick yo' head up out'n de water en tell me Brer Rabbit done gone on by. Oh, no! you ain't de man. I
boun' you ain't. 'Bout dat time, you wuz at home
with yo' fambly, whar you allers is. I dunner whar
you wuz, but I knows whar you is, Brer Bull-frog, en

hit's you en me fer it. Atter de sun goes down dis
day you don't fool no mo' folks gwine 'long dis road.'

"Co'se, Brer Bull-frog dunner w'at Brer B'ar drivin'
at, but he know sump'n hatter be done, en dat mighty
soon, kaze Brer B'ar 'gun to snap his jaws tergedder
en foam at de mouf, en Brer Bull-frog holler out:

"'Oh, pray, Brer B'ar! Lemme off dis time, en I
won't never do so no mo'. Oh, pray, Brer B'ar! do
lemme off dis time, en I'll show you de fattes' bee-
tree in de woods.'

"Ole Brer B'ar, he chomp his toofies en foam at
de mouf. Brer Bull-frog he des up'n squall:

"'Oh, pray, Brer B'ar! I won't never do so no mo'!
Oh, pray, Brer B'ar! Lemme off dis time!'

"But ole Brer B'ar say he gwineter make way wid
'im, en den he sot en study, ole Brer B'ar did, how he
gwineter squench Brer Bull-frog. He know he can't
drown 'im, en he ain't got no fier fer ter bu'n 'im, en
he git mighty pestered. Bimeby ole Brer Bull-frog,
he sorter stop his cryin' en his boo-hooin', en he up'n
say:

"'Ef you gwineter kill me, Brer B'ar, kyar me ter
dat big flat rock out dar on de aidge er de mill-pon',
whar I kin see my fambly, en atter I see um, den you
kin take you axe en sqush me.'

"Dis look so fa'r and squar' dat Brer B'ar he 'gree,
en he take ole Brer Bull-frog by wunner his behime
legs, en sling his axe on his shouder, en off he put fer

de big flat rock. When he git dar he lay Brer Bull-frog down on de rock, en Brer Bull-frog make like he lookin' 'roun' fer his folks. Den Brer B'ar, he draw long breff en pick up his axe. Den he spit in his han's en draw back en come down on de rock—pow!"

"Did he kill the Frog, Uncle Remus?" asked the little boy, as the old man paused to scoop up a thimbleful of glowing embers in his pipe.

" 'Deed, en dat he didn't, honey. 'Twix' de time w'en Brer B'ar raise up wid his axe en w'en he come

down wid it, ole Brer Bull-frog he lipt up en dove down in de mill-pon', kerblink-kerblunk! En w'en he riz way out in de pon' he riz a singin', en dish'yer's de song w'at he sing:

" 'Ingle-go-jang, my joy, my joy—
    Ingle-go-jang, my joy!
I'm right at home, my joy, my joy—
    Ingle-go-jang, my joy!' "

"That's a mighty funny song," said the little boy.

"Funny now, I speck," said the old man, "but 'twern't funny in dem days, en 'twouldn't be funny now ef folks know'd much 'bout de Bull-frog lang-widge ez dey useter. Dat's w'at."

XXV

HOW MR. RABBIT LOST HIS FINE BUSHY TAIL

"One time," said Uncle Remus, sighing heavily and settling himself back in his seat with an air of melancholy resignation—"one time Brer Rabbit wuz gwine 'long down de road shakin' his big bushy tail, en feelin' des ez scrumpshus ez a bee-martin wid a fresh bug." Here the old man paused and glanced at the little boy, but it was evident that the youngster had become so accustomed to the marvelous develop-ments of Uncle Remus's stories, that the extraordi-nary statement made no unusual impression upon him. Therefore the old man began again, and this time in a louder and more insinuating tone:

"One time ole man Rabbit, he wuz gwine 'long down de road shakin' his long, bushy tail, en feelin' mighty biggity."

This was effective.

"Great goodness, Uncle Remus!" exclaimed the little boy in open-eyed wonder, "everybody knows that rabbits haven't got long, bushy tails."

The old man shifted his position in his chair and allowed his venerable head to drop forward until his whole appearance was suggestive of the deepest dejection; and this was intensified by a groan that seemed to be the result of great mental agony. Finally he spoke, but not as addressing himself to the little boy.

"I notices dat dem fokes w'at makes a great 'miration 'bout w'at dey knows is des de fokes w'ich you can't put no 'pennunce in w'en de 'cashun come up. Yer one un um now, en he done come en excuse me er 'lowin dat rabbits is got long, bushy tails, w'ich goodness knows ef I'd a dremp' it, I'd a whirl in en on dremp it."

"Well, but Uncle Remus, you said rabbits had long, bushy tails," replied the little boy. "Now you know you did."

"Ef I ain't fergit it off'n my mine, I say dat ole Brer Rabbit wuz gwine down de big road shakin' his long, bushy tail. Dat w'at I say, en dat I stan's by."

The little boy looked puzzled, but he didn't say
anything. After a while the old man continued:
"Now, den, ef dat's 'greed ter, I'm gwine on, en
ef tain't 'greed ter, den I'm gwineter pick up my cane

en look atter my own intrust. I got wuk lyin' 'roun' yer dat's des natally gittin' moldy."

The little boy still remained quiet, and Uncle Remus proceeded:

"One day Brer Rabbit wuz gwine down de road shakin' his long, bushy tail, w'en who should he strike up wid but ole Brer Fox gwine amblin' long wid a big string er fish! W'en dey pass de time er day wid wunner nudder, Brer Rabbit, he open up de confab, he did, en he ax Brer Fox whar he git dat nice string er fish, en Brer Fox, he up'n 'spon' dat he katch um, en Brer Rabbit, he say whar'bouts, en Brer Fox, he say down at de babtizin' creek, en Brer Rabbit he ax how, kaze in dem days dey wuz monstus fon' er minners, en Brer Fox, he sot down on a log, he did, en he up'n tell Brer Rabbit dat all he gotter do fer ter git er big mess er minners is ter go ter de creek atter sun down, en drap his tail in de water en set dar twel day-light, en den draw up a whole armful er fishes, en dem w'at he don't want, he kin fling back. Right dar's whar Brer Rabbit drap his watermillion, kaze he tuck'n sot out dat night en went a fishin'. De wedder wuz sorter cole, en Brer Rabbit, he got 'im a bottle er dram en put out fer de creek, en w'en he git dar he pick out a good place, en he sorter squot down, he did, en let his tail hang in de water. He sot dar, en he sot dar, en he drunk his dram, en he think he gwineter freeze, but bimeby day come, en dar he wuz. He make a pull, en he feel like he comin' in two, en he fetch nudder jerk, en lo en beholes, whar wuz his tail?"

There was a long pause.

"Did it come off, Uncle Remus?" asked the little boy, presently.

"She did dat!" replied the old man with unction. "She did dat, and dat w'at make all deze yer bob-tail rabbits w'at you see hoppin' en skaddlin' thoo de woods."

"Are they all that way just because the old Rabbit lost his tail in the creek?" asked the little boy.

"Dat's it, honey," replied the old man. "Dat's w'at dey tells me. Look like dey er bleedzd ter take atter der pa."

XXVI

MR. TERRAPIN SHOWS HIS STRENGTH

"Brer Tarrypin wuz de out'nes' man," said Uncle Remus, rubbing his hands together contemplatively, and chuckling to himself in a very significant manner; "he wuz de out'nes' man er de whole gang. He wuz dat."

The little boy sat perfectly quiet, betraying no impatience when Uncle Remus paused to hunt, first in one pocket and then in another, for enough crumbs

of tobacco to replenish his pipe. Presently the old
man proceeded:

"One night Miss Meadows en de gals dey gun a
candy-pullin', en so many er de nabers come in
'sponse ter de invite dat dey hatter put de 'lasses in
de wash pot en b'il' de fier in de yard. Brer B'ar,
he hope * Miss Meadows bring de wood, Brer Fox,

he men' de fier, Brer Wolf, he kep' de dogs off, Brer
Rabbit, he grease de bottom er de plates fer ter keep

* Holp; helped.

de candy fum stickin', en Brer Tarrypin, he klum up
in a cheer, en say he'd watch en see dat de 'lasses
didn't bile over. Dey wuz all dere, en dey wern't
cuttin' up no didos, nudder, kaze Miss Meadows, she
done put her foot down, she did, en say dat w'en
dey come ter her place dey hatter hang up a flag
er truce at de front gate en 'bide by it.

"Well, den, w'iles dey wuz all a settin' dar en de
'lasses wuz a bilin' en a blubberin', dey got ter runnin'
on talkin' mighty biggity. Brer Rabbit, he say he de
swiffes'; but Brer Tarrypin, he rock 'long in de cheer
en watch de 'lasses. Brer Fox, he say he de sharpes',
but Brer Tarrypin he rock 'long. Brer Wolf, he say
he de mos' suvvigus, but Brer Tarrypin, he rock en he
rock 'long. Brer B'ar, he say he de mos' stronges', but
Brer Tarrypin he rock, en he keep on rockin'. Bimeby
he sorter shet one eye, en say, sezee:

" 'Hit look like 'periently dat de ole hardshell ain't
nowhars 'longside er dis crowd, yit yer I is, en I'm de
same man w'at show Brer Rabbit dat he ain't de
swiffes'; en I'm de same man w'at kin show Brer B'ar
dat he ain't de stronges',' sezee.

"Den dey all laff en holler, kaze it look like Brer
B'ar mo' stronger dan a steer. Bimeby, Miss Meadows, she up'n ax, she did, how he gwine do it.

" 'Gimme a good strong rope,' sez Brer Tarrypin,
sezee, 'en lemme git in er puddle er water, en den
let Brer B'ar see ef he kin pull me out,' sezee.

"Den dey all laff g'in, en Brer B'ar, he ups en sez, sezee: 'We ain't got no rope,' sezee.

"'No,' sez Brer Tarrypin, sezee, 'en needer is you got de strenk,' sezee, en den Brer Tarrypin, he rock en rock 'long, en watch de 'lasses a bilin' en a blubberin'.

"Atter w'ile Miss Meadows, she up en say, she did, dat she'd take'n loan de young men her bed-cord, en w'iles de candy wuz a coolin' in de plates, dey could all go ter de branch en see Brer Tarrypin kyar out his projick. Brer Tarrypin," continued Uncle Remus, in a tone at once confidential and argumentative, "wern't much bigger'n de pa'm er my han', en it look mighty funny fer ter year 'im braggin' 'bout how he kin out-pull Brer B'ar. But dey got de bed-cord atter w'ile, en den dey all put out ter de branch. W'en Brer Tarrypin fine de place he wanter, he tuck one een' er de bed-cord, en gun de yuther een' to Brer B'ar.

"'Now den, ladies en gents,' sez Brer Tarrypin, sezee, 'you all go wid Brer B'ar up dar in de woods en I'll stay yer, en w'en you year me holler, den's de time fer Brer B'ar fer ter see ef he kin haul in de slack er de rope. You all take keer er dat ar een',' sezee, 'en I'll take keer er dish yer een',' sezee.

"Den dey all put out en lef' Brer Tarrypin at de branch, en w'en dey got good en gone, he dove down inter de water, he did, en tie de bed-cord hard

en fas' ter wunner deze yer big clay-roots, en den he
riz up en gin a whoop.

"Brer B'ar he wrop de bed-cord roun' his han,' en

wink at de gals, en wid dat he gin a big juk, but Brer
Tarrypin ain't budge. Den he take bof han's en gin
a big pull, but, all de same, Brer Tarrypin ain't budge.
Den he tu'n 'roun', he did, en put de rope cross his
shoulders en try ter walk off wid Brer Tarrypin, but
Brer Tarrypin look like he don't feel like walkin'.
Den Brer Wolf he put in en hope Brer B'ar pull, but
des like he didn't, en den dey all hope 'im, en, bless
grashus! w'iles dey wuz all a pullin', Brer Tarrypin,
he holler, en ax um w'y dey don't take up de slack.

Den w'en Brer Tarrypin feel um quit pullin', he dove
down, he did, en ontie de rope, en by de time dey got
ter de branch, Brer Tarrypin, he wuz settin' in de
aidge er de water des ez natchul ez de nex' un, en he
up'n say, sezee:

"'Dat las' pull er yone wuz a mighty stiff un, en a
leetle mo'n you'd er had me,' sezee. 'Youer monstus
stout, Brer B'ar,' sezee, 'en you pulls like a yoke er
steers, but I sorter had de purchis on you,' sezee.

"Den Brer B'ar, bein's his mouf 'gun ter water
atter de sweetnin,' he up'n say he speck de candy's
ripe, en off dey put atter it!"

"It's a wonder," said the little boy, after a while,
"that the rope didn't break."

"Break who?" exclaimed Uncle Remus, with a
touch of indignation in his tone—"break who? In dem
days, Miss Meadows's bed-cord would a hilt a mule."

This put an end to whatever doubts the child might
have entertained.

XXVII

WHY MR. POSSUM HAS NO HAIR ON HIS TAIL

"Hɪᴛ look like ter me," said Uncle Remus, frown-
ing, as the little boy came hopping and skipping into
the old man's cabin, "dat I see a young un 'bout yo'
size playin' en makin' free wid dem ar chilluns er ole
Miss Favers's yistiddy, en w'en I seed dat, I drap my

axe, en I come in yer en sot flat down right whar
youer settin' now, en I say ter myse'f dat it's 'bout
time fer ole Remus fer ter hang up en quit. Dat's
des zackly w'at I say."

"Well, Uncle Remus, they called me," said the little
boy, in a penitent tone. "They come and called me,
and said they had a pistol and some powder over
there."

"Dar now!" exclaimed the old man, indignantly.
"Dar now! w'at I bin sayin'? Hit's des a born blessin' dat you wa'n't brung home on a litter wid bofe
eyeballs hangin' out en one year clean gone; dat's
w'at 'tis. Hit's des a born blessin'. Hit hope me up
might'ly de udder day w'en I hear Miss Sally layin'
down de law 'bout you en dem Favers chillun, yit, lo
en beholes, de fus news I knows yer you is han'-in-
glove wid um. Hit's nuff fer ter fetch ole Miss right
up out'n dat berryin'-groun' fum down dar in Putmon
County, en w'at yo' gram'ma wouldn't er stood me en
yo' ma ain't gwineter stan' nudder, en de nex time I
hear 'bout sech a come off ez dis, right den en dar
I'm boun' ter lay de case 'fo' Miss Sally. Dem Favers's
wa'n't no 'count 'fo' de war, en dey wa'n't no 'count
endurin' er de war, en dey ain't no 'count atterwards,
en w'iles my head's hot you ain't gwineter go mixin'
up yo'se'f wid de riff-raff er creashun."

The little boy made no further attempt to justify
his conduct. He was a very wise little boy, and he

knew that, in Uncle Remus's eyes, he had been guilty
of a flagrant violation of the family code. Therefore,
instead of attempting to justify himself, he pleaded
guilty, and promised that he would never do so any
more. After this there was a long period of silence,
broken only by the vigorous style in which Uncle
Remus puffed away at his pipe. This was the invariable result. Whenever the old man had occasion
to reprimand the little boy—and the occasions were
frequent—he would relapse into a dignified but stub-
born silence. Presently the youngster drew forth from
his pocket a long piece of candle. The sharp eyes of
the old man saw it at once.

"Don't you come a tellin' me dat Miss Sally gun
you dat," he exclaimed, "kaze she didn't. En I lay
you hatter be monstus sly 'fo' you gotter chance fer
ter snatch up dat piece er cannle."

"Well, Uncle Remus," the little boy explained, "it
was lying there all by itself, and I just thought I'd
fetch it out to you."

"Dat's so, honey," said Uncle Remus, greatly mol-
lified; "dat's so, kaze by now some er dem yuther
niggers 'ud er done had her lit up. Dey er mighty
biggity, dem house niggers is, but I notices dat dey
don't let nuthin' pass. Dey goes 'long wid der han's
en der mouf open, en w'at one don't ketch de tother
one do."

There was another pause, and finally the little boy said:

"Uncle Remus, you know you promised to-day to tell me why the 'Possum has no hair on his tail."

"Law, honey! ain't you done gone en fergot dat off'n yo' mine yit? Hit look like ter me," continued the old man, leisurely refilling his pipe, "dat she sorter run like dis: One time ole Brer Possum, he git so hungry, he did, dat he bleedzd fer ter have a mess er 'simmons. He monstus lazy man, old Brer Possum

wuz, but bimeby his stummick 'gun ter growl en holler at 'im so dat he des hatter rack 'roun' en hunt up sump'n; en w'iles he wuz rackin' 'roun', who sh'd

he run up wid but Brer Rabbit, en dey wuz hail-
fellers, kaze Brer Possum, he ain't bin bodder'n Brer
Rabbit like dem yuther creeturs. Dey sot down by de
side er de big road, en dar dey jabber en confab
'mong wunner nudder, twel bimeby old Brer Possum,
he take 'n tell Brer Rabbit dat he mos' pe'sh out, en
Brer Rabbit, he lip up in de a'r, he did, en smack his
han's tergedder, en say dat he know right whar Brer
Possum kin git a bait er 'simmons. Den Brer Possum,
he say whar, en Brer Rabbit, he say w'ich 'twuz over
at Brer B'ar's 'simmon orchard."

"Did the Bear have a 'simmon orchard, Uncle
Remus?" the little boy asked.

"Co'se, honey, kaze in dem days Brer B'ar wuz a
bee-hunter. He make his livin' findin' bee trees, en de
way he fine um he plant 'im some 'simmon-trees, w'ich
de bees dey'd come ter suck de 'simmons en den ole
Brer B'ar he'd watch um whar dey'd go, en den he'd
be mighty ap' fer ter come up wid um. No matter
'bout dat, de 'simmon patch 'uz dar des like I tell you,
en ole Brer Possum mouf 'gun ter water soon's he
year talk un um, en mos' 'fo' Brer Rabbit done tellin'
'im de news, Brer Possum, he put out, he did, en
'twa'n't long 'fo' he wuz perch up in de highes' tree
in Brer B'ar 'simmon patch. But Brer Rabbit, he
done 'termin' fer ter see some fun, en w'iles all dis 'uz
gwine on, he run 'roun' ter Brer B'ar house, en holler
en tell 'im w'ich dey wuz somebody 'stroyin' un his

'simmons, en Brer B'ar, he hustle off fer ter ketch 'im.

"Eve'y now en den Brer Possum think he year Brer B'ar comin', but he keep on sayin', sezee:

" 'I'll des git one 'simmon mo' en den I'll go; one 'simmon mo' en den I'll go.'

"Las' he year Brer B'ar comin' sho nuff, but 'twuz

de same ole chune—'One 'simmon mo' en den I'll go'
—en des 'bout dat time Brer B'ar busted inter de
patch, en gin de tree a shake, en Brer Possum, he
drapt out longer de yuther ripe 'simmons, but time he
totch de groun' he got his foots tergedder, en he lit
out fer de fence same ez a race-hoss, en 'cross dat
patch him en Brer B'ar had it, en Brer B'ar gain' eve'y
jump, twel time Brer Possum make de fence Brer B'ar
grab 'im by de tail, en Brer Possum, he went out
'tween de rails en gin a powerful juk en pull his tail
out 'twix Brer B'ar tushes; en, lo en beholes, Brer
B'ar hole so tight en Brer Possum pull so hard dat all
de ha'r come off in Brer B'ar's mouf, w'ich, ef Brer
Rabbit hadn't er happen up wid a go'd er water,
Brer B'ar 'der got strankle.

"Fum dat day ter dis," said Uncle Remus, knocking
the ashes carefully out of his pipe, "Brer Possum ain't
had no ha'r on his tail, en needer do his chilluns."

XXVIII

THE END OF MR. BEAR

THE next time the little boy sought Uncle Remus
out, he found the old man unusually cheerful and
good-humoured. His rheumatism had ceased to
trouble him, and he was even disposed to be
boisterous. He was singing when the little boy got
near the cabin, and the child paused on the outside to

listen to the vigorous but mellow voice of the old man, as it rose and fell with the burden of the curiously plaintive song—a senseless affair so far as the words were concerned, but sung to a melody almost thrilling in its sweetness:

> "Han' me down my walkin'-cane
> (Hey my Lily! go down de road!),
> Yo' true lover gone down de lane
> (Hey my Lily! go down de road!)."

The quick ear of Uncle Remus, however, had detected the presence of the little boy, and he allowed his song to run into a recitation of nonsense, of which the following, if it be rapidly spoken, will give a faint idea:

"Ole M'er Jackson, fines' confraction, fell down sta'rs fer to git satisfaction; big Bill Fray, he rule de day, eve'ything he call fer come one, two by three. Gwine 'long one day, met Johnny Huby, ax him grine nine yards er steel fer me, tole me w'ich he couldn't: den I hist 'im over Hickerson Dickerson's barn-doors; knock 'im ninety-nine miles under water, w'en he rise, he rise in Pike straddle un a hanspike, en I lef' 'im dar smokin' er de hornpipe, Juba reda seda breda. Aunt Kate at de gate; I want to eat, she fry de meat en gimme skin, w'ich I fling it back agin. Juba!"

All this, rattled off at a rapid rate and with apparent seriousness, was calculated to puzzle the little boy, and he slipped into his accustomed seat with an expression of awed bewilderment upon his face.

"Hit's all des dat away, honey," continued the old man, with the air of one who had just given an important piece of information. "En w'en you bin cas'n shadders long ez de ole nigger, den you'll fine out who's w'ich, en w'ich's who."

The little boy made no response. He was in thorough sympathy with all the whims and humors of the old man, and his capacity for enjoying them was large enough to include even those he could not understand. Uncle Remus was finishing an axe-handle, and upon these occasions it was his custom to allow the child to hold one end while he applied sand-paper to the other. These relations were pretty soon established, to the mutual satisfaction of the parties most interested, and the old man continued his remarks, but this time not at random:

"W'en I see deze yer swell-head folks like dat 'oman w'at come en tell yo' ma 'bout you chunkin' at her chilluns, w'ich yo ma make Mars John strop you, hit make my mine run back to ole Brer B'ar. Ole Brer B'ar, he got de swell-headedness hisse'f, en ef der wuz enny swinkin', hit swunk too late fer ter he'p ole Brer B'ar. Leas'ways dat's w'at dey tells me, en I ain't never yearn it 'sputed."

"Was the Bear's head sure enough swelled, Uncle Remus?"

"Now you talkin', honey!" exclaimed the old man.

"Goodness! what made it swell?"

This was Uncle Remus's cue. Applying the sandpaper to the axe-helve with gentle vigor, he began:

"One time when Brer Rabbit wuz gwine lopin' home fum a frolic w'at dey bin havin' up at Miss Meadows's, who should he happin up wid but ole Brer B'ar. Co'se, atter w'at done pass 'twix um dey wa'n't no good feelin's 'tween Brer Rabbit en ole Brer B'ar, but Brer Rabbit, he wanter save his manners, en so he holler out:

"Heyo, Brer B'ar! how you come on? I ain't seed you in a coon's age. How all down at yo' house? How Miss Brune en Miss Brindle?"

"Who was that, Uncle Remus?" the little boy interrupted.

"Miss Brune en Miss Brindle? Miss Brune wuz Brer B'ar's ole 'oman, en Miss Brindle wuz his gal. Dat w'at dey call um in dem days. So den Brer Rabbit, he ax him howdy, he did, en Brer B'ar, he 'spon' dat he wuz mighty po'ly, en dey amble 'long, dey did, sorter familious like, but Brer Rabbit, he keep one eye on Brer B'ar, en Brer B'ar, he study how he gwine nab Brer Rabbit. Las' Brer Rabbit, he up'n say, sezee:

"'Brer B'ar, I speck I got some bizness cut out fer you,' sezee.

"'What dat, Brer Rabbit?' sez Brer B'ar, sezee.

"'W'iles I wuz cleanin' up my new-groun' day 'fo' yistiddy,' sez Brer Rabbit, sezee, 'I come 'cross wunner deze yer ole time bee-trees. Hit start holler at de bottom, en stay holler plum der de top, en de honey's des natally oozin' out, en ef you'll drap yo' 'gagements en go 'longer me,' sez Brer Rabbit, sezee, 'you'll git a bait dat'll las' you en yo' fambly twel de middle er nex' mont',' sezee.

"Brer B'ar say he much oblije en he b'leeve he'll go 'long, en wid dat dey put out fer Brer Rabbit's new-groun', w'ich twa'n't so mighty fur. Leas'ways, dey got dar atter w'ile. Ole Brer B'ar, he 'low dat he kin smell de honey. Brer Rabbit, he 'low dat he kin see de honey-koam. Brer B'ar, he 'low dat he can hear de bees a zoonin'. Dey stan' 'roun' en talk biggity, dey did, twel bimeby Brer Rabbit, he up'n say, sezee:

" 'You do de clim-'in', Brer B'ar, en I'll do de rushin' 'roun'; you clime up ter de hole, en I'll take dis yer pine pole en shove de honey up whar you kin git 'er,' sezee.

"Ole Brer B'ar, he spit on his han's en skint up de tree, en jam his head in de hole, en sho nuff, Brer Rabbit, he grab de pine pole, en de way he stir up dem bees wuz sinful—dat's w'at it wuz. Hit wuz sinful. En de bees dey swawm'd on Brer B'ar's head, twel 'fo' he could take it out'n de hole

hit wuz done swell up bigger dan dat dinner-pot, en
dar he swung, en ole Brer Rabbit, he dance 'roun'
en sing:

"'Tree stan' high, but honey mighty sweet—
Watch dem bees wid stingers on der feet.'

"But dar ole Brer B'ar hung, en ef his head ain't
swunk, I speck he hangin' dar yit—dat w'at I speck."

XXIX

MR. FOX GETS INTO SERIOUS BUSINESS

"HIT turn out one time," said Uncle Remus, grind-
ing some crumbs of tobacco between the palms of his
hands, preparatory to enjoying his usual smoke after
supper—"hit turn out one time dat Brer Rabbit make
so free wid de man's collard-patch dat de man he
tuck'n sot a trap fer ole Brer Rabbit."

"Which man was that, Uncle Remus?" asked the
little boy.

"Des a man, honey. Dat's all. Dat's all I knows
—des wunner dese yer mans w'at you see trollopin
'roun' eve'y day. Nobody ain't never year w'at his
name is, en ef dey did dey kep' de news mighty close
fum me. Ef dish yer man is bleedzd fer ter have a
name, den I'm done, kaze you'll hatter go fudder dan
me. Ef you bleedzd ter know mo' dan w'at I duz,
den you'll hatter hunt up some er deze yer niggers

w'at's sprung up sence I commence fer ter shed my ha'r."

"Well, I just thought, Uncle Remus," said the little boy, in a tone remarkable for self-depreciation, "that the man had a name."

"Tooby sho," replied the old man, with unction, puffing away at his pipe. "Co'se. Dat w'at make I say w'at I duz. Dish yer man mout a had a name, en den ag'in he moutn't. He mout er bin name Slipshot Sam, en he mouter bin name ole One-eye Riley, w'ich ef 'twuz hit ain't bin handed roun' ter me. But dish yer man, he in de tale, en w'at we gwine do wid 'im? Dats de p'int, kase w'en I git ter huntin' 'roun' 'mong my 'membunce atter dish yer Mister W'atyoumaycollum's name, she ain't dar. Now den, less des call 'im Mr. Man en let 'im go at dat."

The silence of the little boy gave consent.

"One time," said Uncle Remus, carefully taking up the thread of the story where it had been dropped, "hit turn out dat Brer Rabbit bin makin' so free wid Mr. Man's greens en truck dat Mr. Man, he tuck'n sot a trap for Brer Rabbit, en Brer Rabbit he so greedy dat he tuck'n walk right spang in it, 'fo' he know hisse'f. Well, 'twa'n't long 'fo' yer come Mr. Man, broozin' 'roun', en he ain't no sooner see ole Brer Rabbit dan he smack his han's tergedder en holler out:

" 'Youer nice feller, you is! Yer you bin gobblin'

up my green truck, en now you tryin' ter tote off my
trap. Youer mighty nice chap—dat's w'at you is! But
now dat I got you, I'll des 'bout settle wid you fer de
ole en de new.'

"En wid dat, Mr. Man, he go off, he did, down in
de bushes atter han'ful er switches. Ole Brer Rabbit,
he ain't sayin' nuthin', but he feelin' mighty lonesome,
en he sot dar lookin' like eve'y minnit wuz gwineter
be de nex'. En w'iles Mr. Man wuz off prepa'r'n his
bresh-broom, who should come p'radin' 'long but
Brer Fox. Brer Fox make a great 'miration, he did,
'bout de fix w'at he fine Brer Rabbit in, but Brer Rabbit he make like he fit ter kill hisse'f laffin', en he up'n
tell Brer Fox, he did, dat Miss Meadows's fokes want
'im ter go down ter der house in 'tennunce on a
weddin', en he 'low w'ich he couldn't, en dey 'low
how he could, en den bimeby dey take'n tie 'im dar
w'iles dey go atter de preacher, so he be dar' w'en
dey come back. En mo'n dat, Brer Rabbit up'n tell
Brer Fox dat his chillun's mighty low wid de fever, en
he bleedzd ter go atter some pills fer'm, en he ax
Brer Fox fer ter take his place en go down ter Miss
Meadows's en have nice time wid de gals. Brer Fox,
he in fer dem kinder pranks, en 'twa'n't no time 'fo'
Brer Rabbit had ole Brer Fox harness up dar in his
place, en den he make like he got ter make 'as'e en
git de pills fer dem sick chilluns. Brer Rabbit wa'n't
mo'n out er sight 'fo' yer come Mr. Man wid a han'ful

er hick'ries, but w'en he see Brer Fox tied up dar, he look like he 'stonished.

"'Heyo!' sez Mr. Man, sezee, 'you done change color, en you done got bigger, en yo' tail done grow

out. W'at kin'er w'atzyname is you, ennyhow?' sezee.

"Brer Fox, he stay still, en Mr. Man, he talk on:

"'Hit's mighty big luck,' sezee, 'ef w'en I ketch de chap w'at nibble my greens, likewise I ketch de feller w'at gnyaw my goose,' sezee, en wid dat he let inter Brex Fox wid de hick'ries, en de way he play rap-jacket wuz a caution ter de naberhood. Brer Fox, he

juk en he jump, en he squeal en he squall, but Mr.
Man, he shower down on 'im, he did, like fightin' a
red was'nes'."

The little boy laughed, and Uncle Remus supple-
mented this indorsement of his descriptive powers
with a most infectious chuckle.

"Bimeby," continued the old man, "de switches,
dey got frazzle out, en Mr. Man, he put out atter mo',
en w'en he done got fa'rly outer yearin', Brer Rabbit,
he show'd up, he did, kaze he des bin hidin' out in de
bushes lis'nin' at de racket, en he 'low hit mighty
funny dat Miss Meadows ain't come 'long, kaze he
done bin down ter de doctor house, en dat's fudder
dan de preacher, yit. Brer Rabbit make like he hur-
r'in' on home, but Brer Fox, he open up, he did, en
he say:

"'I thank you fer ter tu'n me loose, Brer Rabbit,
en I'll be 'blije,' sezee, 'kaze you done tie me up so
tight dat it make my head swim, en I don't speck I'd
las' fer ter git ter Miss Meadows's,' sezee.

"Brer Rabbit, he sot down sorter keerless like, en
begin fer ter scratch one year like a man studyin'
'bout sump'n.

"'Dat's so, Brer Fox,' sezee, 'you duz look sorter
stove up. Look like sump'n bin onkoamin' yo' ha'rs,'
sezee.

"Brer Fox ain't sayin' nothin', but Brer Rabbit, he
keep on talkin':

"'Dey ain't no bad feelin's 'twix' us, is dey, Brer Fox? Kaze ef dey is, I ain't got no time fer ter be tarryin' 'roun' yer.'

"Brer Fox say w'ich he don't have no onfrennel-ness, en wid dat Brer Rabbit cut Brer Fox loose des in time fer ter hear Mr. Man w'isserlin up his dogs, en one went one way en de udder went nudder."

XXX

HOW MR. RABBIT SUCCEEDED IN RAISING A DUST

"In dem times," said Uncle Remus, gazing admiringly at himself in a fragment of looking-glass, "Brer Rabbit, en Brer Fox, en Brer Coon, en dem yuther creeturs go co'tin' en sparklin' 'roun' de naberhood mo' samer dan folks. 'Twan't no 'Lemme a hoss,' ner 'Fetch me my buggy,' but dey des up'n lit out en tote deyse'f. Dar's ole Brer Fox, he des wheel 'roun' en fetch his flank one swipe wid 'is tongue en he'd be koam up; en Brer Rabbit, he des spit on his han' en twis' it 'roun' 'mongst de roots er his years en his ha'r'd be roach. Dey wuz dat flirtashus," continued the old man, closing one eye at his image in the glass, "dat Miss Meadows en de gals don't se no peace fum one week een' ter de udder. Chuseday wuz same as Sunday, en Friday wuz same as Chuseday, en hit come down ter dat pass dat w'en Miss Meadows 'ud have chicken-fixins fer dinner, in 'ud drap Brer Fox en Brer Possum, en w'en she'd have fried greens in 'ud pop ole Brer Rabbit, twel 'las' Miss Meadows, she tuck'n tell de gals dat she be dad-blame ef she gwineter keep no tavvum. So dey fix it up 'mong deyse'f, Miss Meadows en de gals did, dat de nex' time de gents call dey'd gin um a game. De gents, dey wuz a co'tin, but Miss Meadows, she don't wanter

marry none un um, en needer duz de gals, en likewise
dey don't wanter have um pester'n 'roun.' Las', one
Chuseday, Miss Meadows, she tole um dat ef dey
come down ter her house de nex' Sat'day evenin', de
whole caboodle un um 'ud go down de road a piece,
whar der wuz a big flint rock, en de man w'at could
take a sludge-hammer en knock de dus' out'n dat
rock, he wuz de man w'at 'ud git de pick er de gals.
Dey all say dey gwine do it, but ole Brer Rabbit, he
crope off whar der wuz a cool
place under some jimson weeds,
en dar he sot wukkin his mind
how he gwineter git dus' out'n
dat rock. Bimeby, w'ile he wuz
a settin' dar, up he jump en
crack his heels tergedder en sing
out:

"'Make a bow ter de Buzzard en
den ter de Crow,
    Takes a limber-toe gemmun fer
    ter jump Jim Crow,'

en wid dat he put out for Brer
Coon house en borrer his slippers. W'en Sat'day evenin' come,
dey wuz all dere. Miss Meadows
en de gals, dey wuz dere; en Brer Coon, en Brer Fox,
en Brer Possum, en Brer Tarrypin, dey wuz dere."

"Where was the Rabbit?" the little boy asked.

"Yuk'n put yo' 'pennunce in ole Brer Rabbit," the old man replied, with a chuckle. "He wuz dere, but he shuffle up kinder late, kaze w'en Miss Meadows en de ballunce un um done gone down ter de place, Brer Rabbit, he crope 'roun' ter de ash-hopper, en fill Brer Coon slippers full er ashes, en den he tuck'n put um on en march off. He got dar atter 'w'ile, en soon's Miss Meadows en de gals seed 'im, dey up'n giggle, en make a great 'miration kaze Brer Rabbit got on slippers. Brer Fox, he so smart, he holler out, he did, en say he lay Brer Rabbit got de groun'-eatch, but Brer Rabbit, he sorter shet one eye, he did, en say, sezee:

"'I bin so useter ridin' hoss-back, ez deze ladies knows, dat I'm gittin' sorter tender-footed;' en dey don't hear much mo' fum Brer Fox dat day, kaze he 'member how Brer Rabbit done bin en rid him; en hit 'uz des 'bout much ez Miss Meadows en de gals could do fer ter keep der snickers fum gittin' up a 'sturbance 'mong de congergashun. But, never mine dat, old Brer Rabbit, he wuz dar, en he so brash dat leetle mo' en he'd er grab up de sludge-hammer en er open up de racket 'fo' ennybody gun de word; but Brer Fox, he shove Brer Rabbit out'n de way en pick up de sludge hisse'f. Now den," continued the old man, with pretty much the air of one who had been the master of similar ceremonies, "de progance wuz dish yer: Eve'y

gent wer ter have th'ee licks at de rock, en de gent
w'at fetch de dus' he were de one w'at gwineter take
de pick er de gals. Ole Brer Fox, he grab de sludge-
hammer, he did, en he come down on de rock—*blim!*

No dus' ain't come. Den he draw back en down he
come ag'in—*blam!* No dus' ain't come. Den he spit in
his han's, en give 'er a big swing en down she come—
kerblap! En yit no dus' ain't flew'd. Den Brer Possum
he make triul, en Brer Coon, en all de ballunce un

um 'cep' Brer Tarrypin, en he 'low dat he got a crick in his neck. Den Brer Rabbit, he grab holt er de sludge, en he lipt up in de a'r en come down on de rock all at de same time—*pow!*—en de ashes, dey flew'd up so, dey did, dat Brer Fox, he tuck'n had a sneezin' spell, en Miss Meadows en de gals dey up'n koff. Th'ee times Brer Rabbit jump up en crack his heels tergedder en come down wid de sludge-hammer—*ker-blam!*—en eve'y time he jump up, he holler out:

" 'Stan' fudder, ladies! Yer come de dus'!' en sho nuff, de dus' come.

"Leas'ways," continued Uncle Remus, "Brer Rabbit got one er de gals, en dey had a weddin' en a big infa'r."

"Which of the girls did the Rabbit marry?" asked the little boy, dubiously.

"I did year tell un 'er name," replied the old man, with a great affectation of interest, "but look like I done gone en fergit it off'n my mine. Ef I don't disremember," he continued, "hit wuz Miss Molly Cottontail, en I speck we better let it go at dat."

XXXI

A PLANTATION WITCH

THE next time the little boy got permission to call upon Uncle Remus, the old man was sitting in his door, with his elbows on his knees and his face buried in his hands, and he appeared to be in great trouble.

"What's the matter, Uncle Remus?" the youngster asked.

"Nuff de matter, honey—mo' dan dey's enny kyo fer. Ef dey ain't some quare gwines on 'roun' dis place I ain't name Remus."

The serious tone of the old man caused the little boy to open his eyes. The moon, just at its full, cast long, vague, wavering shadows in front of the cabin. A colony of tree-frogs somewhere in the distance were treating their neighbors to a serenade, but to the little boy it sounded like a chorus of lost and long-forgotten whistlers. The sound was wherever the im-agination chose to locate it—to the right, to the left, in the air, on the ground, far away or near at hand, but always dim and always indistinct. Something in Uncle Remus's tone exactly fitted all these surround-ings, and the child nestled closer to the old man.

"Yasser," continued Uncle Remus, with an ominous sigh and mysterious shake of the head, "ef dey ain't some quare gwines on in dish yer naberhood, den I'm de ball-headest creetur 'twix' dis en nex' Jinawerry wuz a year 'go, w'ich I knows I ain't. Dat's what."

"What is it, Uncle Remus?"

"I know Mars John bin drivin' Cholly sorter hard ter-day, en I say ter myse'f dat I'd drap 'round 'bout dus' en fling nudder year er corn in de troff en kinder

gin 'im a techin' up wid de kurrier-koam; en bless
grashus! I ain't bin in de lot mo'n a minnit 'fo' I seed
sump'n wuz wrong wid de hoss, and sho' nuff dar
wuz his mane full er witch-stirrups."

"Full of what, Uncle Remus?"

"Full er witch-stirrups, honey. Ain't you seed no
witch-stirrups? Well, w'en you see two stran' er ha'r
tied tergedder in a hoss's mane, dar you see a witch-
stirrup, en, mo'n dat, dat hoss done bin rid by um."

"Do you reckon they have been riding Charley?"
inquired the little boy.

"Co'se, honey. Tooby sho dey is. W'at else dey bin
doin'?"

"Did you ever see a witch, Uncle Remus?"

"Dat ain't needer yer ner dar. W'en I see coon
track in de branch, I know de coon bin 'long dar."

The argument seemed unanswerable, and the little
boy asked, in a confidential tone:

"Uncle Remus, what are
witches like?"

"Dey comes diffunt," re-
sponded the cautious old
darkey. "Dey comes en dey
cunjus fokes. Squinch-owl holler eve'y time he see a witch,
en w'en you hear de dog
howlin' in de middle er de
night, one un um's mighty ap' ter be prowlin' 'roun'.

Cunjun fokes kin tell a witch de minnit dey lays der eyes on it, but dem w'at ain't cunjun, hit's mighty hard ter tell w'en dey see one, kaze dey might come in de 'pearunce un a cow en all kinder creeturs. I ain't

bin useter no cunjun myse'f, but I bin livin' long nuff fer ter know w'en you meets up wid a big black cat in de middle er de road, wid yaller eyeballs, dars yo' witch fresh fum de Ole Boy. En, fuddermo', I know dat 'tain't proned inter no dogs fer ter ketch de rab-

bit w'at use in a berryin'-groun'. Dey er de mos'
ongodlies' creeturs w'at you ever laid eyes on," continued Uncle Remus, with unction. "Down dar in
Putmon County yo' Unk Jeems, he make like he
gwineter ketch wunner dem dar graveyard rabbits.
Sho nuff, out he goes, en de dogs ain't no mo'n got
ter de place fo' up jump de old rabbit right 'mong um,
en atter runnin' 'roun' a time or two, she skip right
up ter Mars Jeems, en Mars Jeems, he des put de
gun-bairl right on 'er en lammed aloose. Hit tored up
de groun' all 'roun', en de dogs, dey rush up, but dey
wa'n't no rabbit dar; but bimeby Mars Jeems, he
seed de dogs tuckin' der tails 'tween der legs, en he
look up, en dar wuz de rabbit caperin' 'roun' on a
toom stone, en wid dat Mars Jeems say he sorter feel
like de time done come w'en yo' gran'ma was 'speck-
tin' un him home, en he call off de dogs en put out.
But dem wuz ha'nts. Witches is deze yer kinder fokes
wat kin drap der body en change inter a cat en a
wolf en all kinder creeturs."

"Papa says there ain't any witches," the little boy
interrupted.

"Mars John ain't live long ez I is," said Uncle
Remus, by way of comment. "He ain't bin broozin'
'roun' all hours er de night en day. I know'd a nigger
w'ich his brer wuz a witch, kaze he up'n tole me how
he tuck'n kyo'd 'im; en he kyo'd 'im good, mon."

"How was that?" inquired the little boy.

"Hit seem like," continued Uncle Remus, "dat witch fokes is got a slit in de back er de neck, en w'en dey wanter change derse'f, dey des pull de hide over der head same ez if 'twuz a shut, en dar dey is."

"Do they get out of their skins?" asked the little boy, in an awed tone.

"Tooby sho, honey. You see yo' pa pull his shut off? Well, dat dez 'zackly de way dey duz. But dish yere nigger w'at I'm tellin' you 'bout, he kyo'd his brer de v'ey fus pass he made at him. Hit got so dat fokes in de settlement didn't have no peace. De chil·luns 'ud wake up in de mawnins wid der ha'r tangle up, en wid scratches on um like dey bin thoo a brier-patch, twel bimeby one day de nigger he 'low dat he'd set up dat night en keep one eye on his brer; en sho' nuff dat night, des ez de chickens wuz crowin' fer twelve, up jump de brer and pull off his skin en sail out'n de house in de shape un a bat, en w'at duz de nigger do but grab up de hide, and turn it wrong-sudout'ards en sprinkle it wid salt. Den he lay down en watch fer ter see w'at de news wuz gwineter be. Des 'fo' day yer come a big black cat in de do', en de nigger git up, he did, en druv her away. Bimeby, yer come a big black dog snuffin' roun', en de nigger up wid a chunk en lammed 'im side er de head. Den a squinch-owl lit on de koam er de house, en de nigger jam de shovel in de fier en make 'im flew away.

Las', yer come a great big black wolf wid his eyes
shinin' like fier coals, en he grab de hide and rush out.
'Twa'n't long 'fo' de nigger year his brer holler'n en
squallin', en he tuck a light, he did, en went out, en
dar wuz his brer des a waller'n on de groun' en
squirmin' 'roun', kaze de salt on de skin wuz stingin'
wuss'n ef he had his britches lineded wid yaller-
jackets. By nex' mawnin' he got so he could sorter
shuffle 'long, but he gun up cunjun, en ef dere wuz
enny mo' witches in dat settlement dey kep' mighty
close, en dat nigger he ain't skunt hisse'f no mo' not.
endurin' er my 'membunce."

The result of this was that Uncle Remus had to
take the little boy by the hand and go with him to
the "big house," which the old man was not loath to
do; and, when the child went to bed, he lay awake a
long time expecting an unseemly visitation from
some mysterious source. It soothed him, however, to
hear the strong, musical voice of his sable patron, not
very far away, tenderly contending with a lusty tune;
and to this accompaniment the little boy dropped
asleep:

"Hit's eighteen hunder'd, forty-en-eight,
    Christ done made dat crooked way straight—
        En I don't wanter stay here no longer;
    Hit's eighteen hunder'd, forty-en-nine,
    Christ done turn dat water inter wine—
        En I don't wanter stay here no longer."

XXXII

"JACKY-MY-LANTERN" *

UPON his next visit to Uncle Remus, the little boy
was exceedingly anxious to know more about witches,
but the old man prudently refrained from exciting the
youngster's imagination any further in that direction.
Uncle Remus had a board across his lap, and, armed
with a mallet and a shoe-knife, was engaged in making shoe-pegs.

"W'iles I wuz crossin' de branch des now," he said,
endeavoring to change the subject, "I come up wid a
Jacky-my-lantern, en she wuz bu'nin' wuss'n a bunch
er lightnin'-bugs, mon. I know'd she wuz a fixin' fer
ter lead me inter dat quogmire down in de swamp,
en I steer'd cle'r un' er. Yasser. I did dat. You ain't
never seed no Jacky-my-lanterns, is you, honey?"

The little boy never had, but he had heard of them,
and he wanted to know what they were, and thereupon Uncle Remus proceeded to tell him.

"One time," said the old darkey, transferring his
spectacles from his nose to the top of his head and

---

* This story is popular on the coast and among the rice-planta-
tions, and, since the publication of some of the animal-myths in the
newspapers, I have received a version of it from a planter in south-
west Georgia; but it seems to me to be an intruder among the
genuine myth-stories of the negroes. It is a trifle too elaborate.
Nevertheless, it is told upon the plantations with great gusto, and
there are several versions in circulation.

leaning his elbows upon his peg-board, "dere wuz a blacksmif man, en dish yer blacksmif man, he tuck'n stuck closer by his dram dan he did by his bellus. Monday mawnin' he'd git on a spree, en all dat week he'd be on a spree, en de nex' Monday mawnin' he'd take a fresh start. Bimeby, one day, atter de blacksmif bin spreein' 'roun' en cussin' might'ly, he hear a sorter rustlin' fuss at de do', en in walk de Bad Man."

"Who, Uncle Remus?" the little boy asked.

"De Bad Man, honey; de Ole Boy hisse'f right fresh from de ridjun w'at you year Miss Sally readin' 'bout. He done hide his hawns, en his tail, en his hoof, en he come dress up like w'ite fokes. He tuck off his hat en he bow, en den he tell de blacksmif who he is, en dat he done come atter 'im. Den de blacksmif, he gun ter cry en beg, en he beg so hard en he cry so loud dat de Bad Man say he make a trade wid 'im. At de een' er one year de sperit er de blacksmif wuz to be his'n en endurin' er dat time de blacksmif mus' put in his hottes' licks in de intruss er de Bad Man, en den he put a spell on de cheer de blacksmif was settin' in, en on his sludge-hammer. De man w'at sot in de cheer couldn't git up less'n de blacksmif let 'im, en de man w'at pick up de sludge 'ud hatter keep on knockin' wid it twel de blacksmif say quit; en den he gun 'im money plenty, en off he put.

"De blacksmif, he sail in fer ter have his fun, en he have so much dat he done clean forgot 'bout his con-

track, but bimeby, one day he look down de road, en
dar he see de Bad Man comin', en den he know'd de

year wuz out. W'en de Bad Man got in de do', de
blacksmif wuz poundin' 'way at a hoss-shoe, but he
wa'n't so bizzy dat he didn't ax 'im in. De Bad Man
sorter do like he ain't got no time fer ter tarry, but de
blacksmif say he got some little jobs dat he bleedzd
ter finish up, en den he ax de Bad Man fer ter set
down a minnit; en de Bad Man, he tuck'n sot down,

en he sot in dat cheer w'at he done conju'd en, co'se,
dar he wuz. Den de blacksmif, he 'gun ter poke fun
at de Bad Man, en he ax him don't he want a dram,
en won't he hitch his cheer up little nigher de fier,
en de Bad Man, he beg en he beg, but 'twan't doin'
no good, kase de blacksmif 'low dat he gwineter keep
'im dar twel he promus dat he let 'im off one year mo',
en, sho nuff, de Bad Man promus dat ef de blacksmif let 'im up he give 'im a n'er showin'. So den de
blacksmif gun de wud, en de Bad Man sa'nter off
down de big road, settin' traps en layin' his progance
fer ter ketch mo' sinners.

"De nex' year hit pass same like t'er one. At de
'p'inted time yer come de Ole Boy atter de blacksmif,
but still de blacksmif had some jobs dat he bleedzd ter
finish up, en he ax de Bad Man fer ter take holt er de
sludge en he he'p 'im out; en de Bad Man, he 'low dat
r'er'n be disperlite, he don't keer ef he do hit 'er a biff
er two; en wid dat he grab up de sludge, en dar he
wuz 'gin, kase he done conju'd de sludge so dat who-
somedever tuck 'er up can't put 'er down less'n de
blacksmif say de wud. Dey perlaver'd dar, dey did,
twel bimeby de Bad Man he up'n let 'im off n'er year.

"Well, den, dat year pass same ez t'er one. Mont'
in en mont' out dat man wuz rollin' in dram, en
bimeby yer come de Bad Man. De blacksmif cry en
he holler, en he rip 'roun' en t'ar his ha'r, but hit des
like he didn't, kase de Bad Man grab 'im up en cram

'im in a bag en tote 'im off. W'iles dey wuz gwine 'long dey come up wid a passel er fokes w'at wuz havin' wunner deze yer fote er July bobbycues, en de Ole Boy, he 'low dat maybe he kin git some mo' game, en w'at do he do but jine in wid um. He jines in en he talk politics same like t'er fokes, twel bimeby dinnertime come 'roun', en dey ax 'im up, w'ich 'greed wid his stummuck, en he pozzit his bag underneed de table 'longside de udder bags w'at de hongry fokes'd brung.

"No sooner did de blacksmif git back on de groun' dan he 'gun ter wuk his way outer de bag. He crope out, he did, en den he tuck'n change de bag. He tuck'n tuck a n'er bag en lay it down whar dish yer bag wuz, en den he crope outer de crowd en lay low in de underbresh.

"Las', w'en de time come fer ter go, de Ole Boy up wid his bag en slung her on his shoulder, en off he put fer de Bad Place. W'en he got dar he tuck'n drap de bag off'n his back en call up de imps, en dey des come a squallin' en a caperin', w'ich I speck dey mus' a bin hongry. Leas'ways dey des swawm'd 'roun', hollerin' out:

" 'Daddy, w'at you brung—daddy, w'at you brung?'

"So den dey open de bag, en lo en beholes, out jump a big bull-dog, en de way he shuck dem little imps wuz a caution, en he kep' on gnyawin' un um twel de Ole Boy open de gate en t'un 'im out."

"And what became of the blacksmith?" the little boy asked, as Uncle Remus paused to snuff the candle with his fingers.

"I'm drivin' on 'roun', honey. Atter 'long time, de blacksmif he tuck'n die, en w'en he go ter de Good Place de man at de gate dunner who he is, en he can't squeeze in. Den he go down ter de Bad Place, en knock. De Ole Boy, he look out, he did, en he know'd de blacksmif de minnit he laid eyes on 'im; but he shake his head en say, sezee:

" 'You'll hatter skuze me, Brer Blacksmif, kase I dun had 'speunce 'longer you. You'll hatter go some'rs else ef you wanter raise enny racket,' sezee, en wid dat he shet do do'.

"En dey do say," continued Uncle Remus, with unction, "dat sense dat day de blacksmif bin sorter huv'rin' 'roun' 'twix' de heavens en de ye'th, en dark nights he shine out so fokes call 'im Jacky-my-lantun. Dat's w'at dey tells me. Hit

may be wrong er't maybe right, but dat's w'at I
years.

XXXIII

WHY THE NEGRO IS BLACK

ONE night, while the little boy was watching Uncle
Remus twisting and waxing some shoe-thread, he
made what appeared to him to be a very curious dis-
covery. He discovered that the palms of the old
man's hands were as white as his own, and the fact
was such a source of wonder that he at last made it
the subject of remark. The response of Uncle Remus
led to the earnest recital of a piece of unwritten history that must prove interesting to ethnologists.

"Tooby sho de pa'm er my han's w'ite, honey," he
quietly remarked, "en, w'en it come ter dat, dey wuz
a time w'en all de w'ite folks 'uz black—blacker dan
me, kaze I done bin yer so long dat I bin sorter
bleach out."

The little boy laughed. He thought Uncle Remus
was making him the victim of one of his jokes; but
the youngster was never more mistaken. The old
man was serious. Nevertheless, he failed to rebuke
the ill-timed mirth of the child, appearing to be altogether engrossed in his work. After a while, he resumed:

"Yasser. Fokes dunner w'at bin yit, let 'lone w'at

gwinter be. Niggers is niggers now, but de time wuz w'en we 'uz all niggers tergedder."

"When was that, Uncle Remus?"

"Way back yander. In dem times we 'uz all un us black; we 'uz all niggers tergedder, en 'cordin' ter all de 'counts w'at I years fokes 'uz gittin' 'long 'bout ez well in dem days ez dey is now. But atter 'w'ile de news come dat dere wuz a pon' er water some'rs in de naberhood, w'ich ef dey'd git inter dey'd be wash off nice en w'ite, en den one un um, he fine de place en make er splunge inter de pon', en come out w'ite ez a town gal. En den, bless grashus! w'en de fokes seed it, dey make a break fer de pon', en dem w'at wuz de soopless, dey got in fus' en dey come out w'ite; en dem w'at wuz de nex' soopless, dey got in nex', en dey come out merlatters; en dey wuz sech a crowd un um dat dey mighty nigh use de water up, w'ich w'en dem yuthers come 'long, de morest dey could do wuz ter paddle about wid der foots en dabble in it wid der han's. Dem wuz de niggers, en down ter dis day dey ain't no w'ite 'bout a nigger 'ceppin de pa'ms er der han's en de soles er der foot."

The little boy seemed to be very much interested in this new account of the origin of races, and he made some further inquiries, which elicited from Uncle Remus the following additional particulars:

"De Injun en de Chinee got ter be 'counted 'long er de merlatter. I ain't seed no Chinee dat I knows un, but dey tells me dey er sorter 'twix' a brown en a brindle. Dey er all merlatters."

"But mamma says the Chinese have straight hair," the little boy suggested.

"Co'se, honey," the old man unhesitatingly responded, "dem w'at git ter de pon' time nuff fer ter git der head in de water, de water hit onkink der ha'r. Hit bleedzd ter be dat away."

XXXIV

THE SAD FATE OF MR. FOX

"Now, den," said Uncle Remus, with unusual gravity, as soon as the little boy, by taking his seat, announced that he was ready for the evening's entertainment to begin; "now, den, dish yer tale w'at I'm agwine ter gin you is de las' row er stumps, sho. Dish yer's whar ole Brer Fox los' his breff, en he ain't fine it no mo' down ter dis day."

"Did he kill himself, Uncle Remus?" the little boy asked, with a curious air of concern.

"Hole on dar, honey!" the old man exclaimed, with a great affectation of alarm; "hole on dar! Wait! Gimme room! I don't wanter tell you no story, en ef you keep shovin' me forrerd, I mout git some er de facks mix up 'mong deyse'f. You gotter gimme room en you gotter gimme time."

The little boy had no other premature questions

to ask, and, after a pause, Uncle Remus resumed:
"Well, den, one day Brer Rabbit go ter Brer Fox
house, he did, en he put up mighty po' mouf. He say
his ole 'oman sick, en his chilluns cole, en de fier done
gone out. Brer Fox, he feel bad 'bout dis, en he tuck'n
s'ply Brer Rabbit widder chunk er fier. Brer Rabbit
see Brer Fox cookin' some nice beef, en his mouf gun
ter water, but he take de fier, he did, en he put out
to'rds home; but present'y yer he come back, en he
say de fier done gone out. Brer Fox 'low dat he want
er invite to dinner, but he don't say nuthin', en
bimeby Brer Rabbit he up'n say, sezee:

" 'Brer Fox, whar you git so much nice beef?'
sezee, en den Brer Fox he up'n 'spon', sezee:

" 'You come ter my house ter-morrer ef yo' fokes
ain't too sick, en I kin show you whar you kin git
plenty beef mo' nicer dan dish yer,' sezee.

"Well, sho nuff, de nex' day fotch Brer Rabbit, en
Brer Fox say, sezee:

" 'Der's a man down yander by Miss Meadows's
w'at got heap er fine cattle, en he gotter cow name
Bookay,' sezee, 'en you des go en say *Bookay*, en
she'll open her mouf, en you kin jump in en git des
as much meat ez you kin tote,' sez Brer Fox, sezee.

" 'Well, I'll go 'long,' sez Brer Rabbit, sezee, 'en
you kin jump fus' en den I'll come follerin' atter,'
sezee.

"Wid dat dey put out, en dey went promernadin'

'roun' 'mong de cattle, dey did, twel bimeby dey struck up wid de one dey wuz atter. Brer Fox, he up,

he did, en holler *Bookay,* en de cow flung 'er mouf wide open. Sho nuff, in dey jump, en w'en dey got dar, Brer Fox, he say, sezee:

"'You kin cut mos' ennywheres, Brer Rabbit, but don't cut 'round' de haslett,' sezee.

"Den Brer Rabbit, he holler back, he did: 'I'm a gitten me out a roas'n-piece,' sezee.

"'Roas'n, er bakin', er fryin',' sez Brer Fox, sezee, 'don't git too nigh de haslett,' sezee.

"Dey cut en dey kyarved, en dey kyarved en dey cut, en w'iles dey wuz cuttin' en kyarvin', en slashin' 'way, Brer Rabbit, he tuck'n hacked inter de haslett, en wid dat down fell de cow dead.

" 'Now, den,' sez Brer Fox, 'we er gone, sho,' sezee.

" 'W'at we gwine do?' sez Brer Rabbit, sezee.

" 'I'll git in de maul,' sez Brer Fox, 'en you'll jump in de gall,' sezee.

"Nex' mawnin' yer cum de man w'at de cow b'long ter, and he ax who kill Bookay. Nobody don't say nuthin'. Den de man say he'll cut 'er open en see, en den he whirl in, en twan't no time 'fo' he had 'er intruls spread out. Brer Rabbit, he crope out'n de gall, en say, sezee:

" 'Mister Man! Oh, Mister Man! I'll tell you who kill yo' cow. You look in de maul, en dar you'll fine 'im,' sezee.

"Wid dat de man tuck a stick and lam down on de maul so hard dat he kill Brer Fox stone-dead. W'en Brer Rabbit see Brer Fox wuz laid out fer good, he make like he mighty sorry, en he up'n ax de man fer Brer Fox head. Man say he ain't keerin', en den Brer Rabbit tuck'n brung it ter Brer Fox house. Dar he see ole Miss Fox, en he tell 'er dat he done fotch her some nice beef w'at 'er ole man sont 'er, but she ain't gotter look at it twel she go ter eat it.

"Brer Fox son wuz name Tobe, en Brer Rabbit tell Tobe fer ter keep still w'iles his mammy cook de nice beef w'at his daddy sont 'im. Tobe he wuz mighty

hongry, en he look in de pot he did w'iles de cookin'
wuz gwine on, en dar he see his daddy head, en wid
dat he sot up a howl en tole his mammy. Miss Fox,
she git mighty mad w'en she fine she cookin' her ole
man head, en she call up de dogs, she did, en sickt
'em on Brer Rabbit; en ole Miss Fox en Tobe en de
dogs, dey push Brer Rabbit so close dat he hatter
take a holler tree. Miss Fox, she tell Tobe fer ter stay
dar en mine Brer Rabbit, w'ile she goes en git de ax,
en w'en she gone, Brer Rabbit, he tole Tobe ef he go
ter de branch en git 'im a drink er water dat he'll gin
'im a dollar. Tobe, he put out, he did, en bring some
water in his hat, but by de time he got back Brer
Rabbit done out en gone. Ole Miss Fox, she cut and
cut twel down come de tree, but no Brer Rabbit dar.
Den she lay de blame on Tobe, en she say she gwineter
lash 'im, en Tobe, he put out en run, de ole 'oman
atter 'im. Bimeby, he come up wid Brer Rabbit, en
sot down fer to tell 'im how 'twuz, en w'iles dey wuz
a settin' dar, yer come ole Miss Fox a slippin' up en
grab um bofe. Den she tell um w'at she gwine do.
Brer Rabbit she gwineter kill, en Tobe she gwineter
lam ef its de las' ack. Den Brer Rabbit sez, sezee:

" 'Ef you please, ma'am, Miss Fox, lay me on de
grinestone en groun' off my nose so I can't smell no
mo' w'en I'm dead.'

"Miss Fox, she tuck dis ter be a good idee, en she
fotch bofe un um ter de grinestone, en set um up on

it so dat she could groun' off Brer Rabbit nose. Den
Brer Rabbit, he up'n say, sezee:

"'Ef you please, ma'am, Miss Fox, Tobe he kin

turn de handle w'iles you goes atter some water fer
ter wet de grinestone,' sezee.

"Co'se, soon'z Brer Rabbit see Miss Fox go atter
de water, he jump down en put out, en dis time he
git clean away."

"And was that the last of the Rabbit, too, Uncle
Remus?" the little boy asked, with something like
a sigh.

"Don't push me too close, honey," responded the old man; "don't shove me up in no cornder. I don't wanter tell you no stories. Some say dat Brer Rabbit's ole 'oman died fum eatin' some pizen-weed, en dat Brer Rabbit married ole Miss Fox, en some say not. Some tells one tale en some tells nudder; some say da fum dat time forrer'd de Rabbits en de Foxes make fren's en stay so; some say dey kep on quollin'. Hit look like it mixt. Let dem tell you w'at knows. Dat w'at I years you gits it straight like I yeard it."

There was a long pause, which was finally broken by the old man:

"Hit's 'gin de rules fer you ter be noddin' yer, honey. Bimeby you'll drap off en I'll hatter tote you up ter de big 'ouse. I hear dat baby cryin', en bimeby Miss Sally'll fly up en be a holler'n atter you."

"Oh, I wasn't asleep," the little boy replied. "I was just thinking."

"Well, dat's diffunt," said the old man. "Ef you'll clime up on my back," he continued, speaking softly, "I speck I ain't too ole fer ter be yo' hoss fum yer ter de house. Many en many's de time dat I toted yo' Unk Jeems dat away, en Mars Jeems wuz heavier sot dan w'at you is."

PLANTATION PROVERBS

Big 'possum clime little tree.
Dem w'at eats kin say grace.
Ole man Know-All died las' year.
Better de gravy dan no grease 'tall.
Dram ain't good twel you git it.
Lazy fokes' stummucks don't git tired.
Rheumatiz don't he'p at de log-rollin'.

Mole don't see w'at his naber doin'.

Save de pacin' mar' fer Sunday.

Don't rain eve'y time de pig squeal.

Crow en corn can't grow in de same fiel'.

Tattlin' 'oman can't make de bread rise.

Rails split 'fo' bre'kfus' 'll season de dinner.

Dem w'at knows too much sleeps under de ash-hopper.

Ef you wanter see yo' own sins, clean up a new groun'.

Hog dunner w'ich part un 'im'll season de turnip salad.

Hit's a blessin' de w'ite sow don't shake de plum-tree.

Winter grape sour, whedder you kin reach 'im or not.

Mighty po' bee dat don't make mo' honey dan he want.

Kwishins on mule's foots done gone out er fashun.

Pigs dunno w'at a pen's fer.

Possum's tail good as a paw.

Dogs don't bite at de front gate.

Colt in de barley-patch kick high.

Jay-bird don't rob his own nes'.

Pullet can't roost too high for de owl.

Meat fried 'fo' day won't las' twel night.

Stump water won't kyo de gripes.

De howlin' dog know w'at he sees.

Bline hoss don't fall w'en he follers de bit.

Hongry nigger won't w'ar his maul out.

Don't fling away de empty wallet.

Black-snake know de way ter de hin nes'.

Looks won't do ter split rails wid.

Settin' hens don't hanker arter fresh aigs.

Tater-vine growin' w'ile you sleep.

Hit take two birds fer to make a nes'.

Ef you bleedzd ter eat dirt, eat clean dirt.

Tarrypin walk fast 'nuff fer to go visitin'.

Empty smoke-house makes de pullet holler.

W'en coon take water he fixin' fer ter fight.

Corn makes mo' at de mill dan it does in de crib.

Good luck say: "Op'n yo' mouf en shet yo' eyes."

Nigger dat gets hurt wukkin oughter show de skyars.

Fiddlin' nigger say hit's long ways ter de dance.

Rooster makes mo' racket dan de hin w'at lay de aig.

Meller mush-million hollers at you fum over de fence.

Nigger wid a pocket-han'kcher better be looked atter.

Rain-crow don't sing no chune, but youk'n 'pen' on 'im.

One-eyed mule can't be handled on de bline side.

Moon may shine, but a lightered knot's mighty handy.

Licker talks mighty loud w'en it git loose fum de jug.

De proudness un a man don't count w'en his head's cold.

Hongry rooster don't cackle w'en he fine a wum.

Some niggers mighty smart, but dey can't drive de pidgins ter roos'.

You may know de way, but better keep yo' eyes on de seven stairs.

All de buzzards in de settlement 'll come to de gray mule's funer'l.

Youk'n hide de fier, but w'at you gwine do wid de smoke?

Ter-morrow may be de carridge-driver's day for ploughin'.

Hit's a mighty deaf nigger dat don't year de dinner-ho'n.

Hit takes a bee fer ter git de sweetness out'n de hoar-houn' blossom.

Ha'nts don't bodder longer hones' folks, but you better go 'roun' de grave-yard.

De pig dat runs off wid de year er corn gits little mo' dan de cob.

Sleepin' in de fence-cornder don't fetch Chrismus in de kitchen.

De spring-house may freeze, but de niggers 'll keep de shuck-pen warm.

'Twix' de bug en de bee-martin 'tain't hard ter tell w'ich gwineter git kotch.

Don't 'sput wid de squinch-owl. Jam de shovel in de fier.

You'd see mo' er de mink ef he know'd whar de yard dog sleeps.

Troubles is seasonin'. 'Simmons ain't good twel dey 'er fros'-bit.

Watch out w'en you'er gittin all you want. Fat tenin' hogs ain't in luck.

HIS SONGS

I

REVIVAL HYMN

Oh, whar shill we go w'en de great
    day comes,
    Wid de blowin' er de trumpits en de
      bangin' er de drums?
How many po' sinners'll be kotched out late
En fine no latch ter de golden gate?
    No use fer ter wait twel ter-morrer!
    De sun musn't set on yo' sorrer,
    Sin's ez sharp ez a bamboo-brier—
    Oh, Lord! fetch de mo'ners up higher!

W'en de nashuns er de earf is a stan'in all aroun',
Who's a gwineter be choosen fer ter w'ar de glory-
    crown?
Who's a gwine fer ter stan' stiff-kneed en bol'.
En answer to der name at de callin' er de roll?
    You better come now ef you comin'—
    Ole Satun is loose en a bummin'—
    De wheels er distruckshun is a hummin'—
    Oh, come 'long, sinner, ef you comin'!

De song er salvashun is a mighty sweet song,
En de Pairidise win' blow fur en blow strong,
En Aberham's bosom, hit's saft en hit's wide,
En right dar's de place whar de sinners oughter hide!
    Oh, you nee'nter be a stoppin' en a lookin';
    Ef you fool wid ole Satun you'll git took in;
    You'll hang on de aidge en get shook in,
    Ef you keep on a stoppin' en a lookin'.

De time is right now, en dish yer's de place—
Let de sun er salvashun shine squar' in yo' face;
Fight de battles er de Lord, fight soon en fight late,
En you'll allers fine a latch ter de golden gate.
    No use fer ter wait twel ter-morrer,
    De sun musn't set on yo' sorrer—
    Sin's ez sharp ez a bamboo-brier,
    Ax de Lord fer ter fetch you up higher!

II

CAMP-MEETING SONG *

OH, de worril is roun' en de worril is wide—
Lord! 'member deze chillun in de mornin'—

---

* In the days of slavery, the religious services held by the
negroes who accompanied their owners to the camp-meetings were
marvels of earnestness and devotion.

Hit's a mighty long ways up de mountain side,
  En dey ain't no place fer dem sinners fer ter hide,
  En dey ain't no place whar sin kin abide,
    W'en de Lord shill come in de mornin'!
      Look up en look aroun',
      Fling yo' burden on de groun',
      Hit's a gittin' mighty close on ter mornin'!
      Smoove away sin's frown—
      Retch up en git de crown,
      W'at de Lord will fetch in de mornin'!

De han' er ridem'shun, hit's hilt out ter you—
  Lord! 'member dem sinners in de mornin'!
Hit's a mighty pashent han', but de days is but few,
W'en Satun, he'll come a demandin' un his due,
En de stiff-neck sinners 'll be smotin' all fru—
  Oh, you better git ready fer de mornin'!
      Look up en set yo' face
      Todes de green hills er grace
      'Fo' de sun rises up in de mornin'—
      Oh, you better change yo' base,
      Hits yo' soul's las' race
      Fer de glory dat's a comin' in de mornin'!

De farmer gits ready w'en de lan's all plowed
  Fer ter sow dem seeds in de mornin'—
De sperrit may be puny en de flesh may be proud,
But you better cut loose fum de scoffin' crowd,

En jine dese Christuns w'at's a cryin' out loud
Fer de Lord fer ter come in de mornin'!
    Shout loud en shout long,
    Let de ekkoes ans'er strong,
W'en de sun rises up in de mornin'!
    Oh, you allers will be wrong
    Twel you choose ter belong
Ter de Marster w'at's a comin' in de mornin'!

III

CORN-SHUCKING SONG

Oh, de fus news you know de day'll be a breakin'—
    (Hey O! Hi O! Up'n down de Bango! *)
An' de fier be a burnin' en' de ash-cake a bakin',
    (Hey O! Hi O! Up'n down de Bango!)
An' de hen'll be a hollerin' en de boss 'll be a wakin'—
    (Hey O! Hi O! Up'n down de Bango!)
Better git up, nigger, en give yo'se'f a shakin'—
    (Hi O, Miss Sindy Ann!)

Oh, honey! w'en you see dem ripe stars a fallin'—
    (Hey O! Hi O! Up'n down de Bango!)

---

* So far as I know, "Bango" is a meaningless term, introduced
on account of its sonorous ruggedness.

Oh, honey! w'en you year de rain-crow a callin'—
    (Hey O! Hi O! Up'n down de Bango!)
Oh, honey! w'en you year dat red calf a bawlin'—
    (Hey O! Hi O! Up'n down de Bango!)
Den de day time's, a creepin' en a crawlin'—
    (Hi O, Miss Sindy Ann!)

Fer de los' ell en yard * is a huntin' fer de mornin',
    (Hi O! git 'long! go 'way!)
En she'll ketch up widdus 'fo' we ever git dis corn in—
    (Oh, go 'way, Sindy Ann!)

Oh, honey! w'en you year dat tin horn a tootin'—
    (Hey O! Hi O! Up'n down de Bango!)
Oh, honey, w'en you year de squinch owl a hootin'—
    (Hey O! Hi O! Up'n down de Bango!)
Oh, honey! w'en you year dem little pigs a rootin'—
    (Hey O! Hi O! Up'n down de Bango!)
Right den she's a comin' a skippin' en a scootin'—
    (Hi O, Miss Sindy Ann!)

Oh, honey, w'en you year dat roan mule whicker—
    (Hey O! Hi O! Up'n down de Bango!)
W'en you see Mister Moon turnin' pale en gittin'
    sicker—
    (Hey O! Hi O! Up'n down de Bango!)

---

* The sword and belt in the constellation of Orion.

Den hit's time fer ter handle dat corn a little quicker—
    (Hey O! Hi O! Up'n down de Bango!)
Ef you wanter git a smell er old Marster's jug er
    licker—
    (Hi O, Miss Sindy Ann!)

Fer de los' ell en yard is a huntin' fer de mornin'
    (Hi O! git 'long! go 'way!)
En she'll ketch up widdus 'fo' we ever git dis corn in—
    (Oh, go 'way, Sindy Ann!)
You niggers 'cross dar! you better stop your dancin'—
    (Hey O! Hi O! Up'n down de Bango!)
No use fer ter come a flingin' un yo' "sha'n'ts" in—
    (Hey O! Hi O! Up'n down de Bango!)
No use fer ter come a flingin' un yo' "can't's" in—
    (Hey O! Hi O! Up'n down de Bango!)
Kaze dey ain't no time fer yo' pattin' ner yo' prancin'!
    (Hi O, Miss Sindy Ann!)

Mr. Rabbit see de Fox, en he sass um en jaws um—
    (Hey O! Hi O! Up'n down de Bango!)
Mr. Fox ketch de Rabbit, en he scratch um en he
    claws um—
    (Hey O! Hi O! Up'n down de Bango!)
En he tar off de hide, en he chaws um en he gnyaws
    um—
    (Hey O! Hi O! Up'n down de Bango!)
Same like gal chawin' sweet gum en rozzum—
    (Hi O, Miss Sindy Ann!)

Fer de los' ell en yard is a huntin' fer de mornin'
    (Hi O! git 'long! go 'way!)
En she'll ketch up widdus 'fo' we ever git dis corn in
    (Oh, go 'way, Sindy Ann!)

Oh, work on, boys! give deze shucks a mighty
      wringin'—
    (Hey O! Hi O! Up'n down de Bango!)
'Fo' de boss come aroun' a dangin' en a dingin'—
    (Hey O! Hi O! Up'n down de Bango!)

Git up en move aroun'! set dem big han's ter swingin'—
    (Hey O! Hi O! Up'n down de Bango!)
Git up'n shout loud! let de w'ite folks year you singin'!
    (Hi O, Miss Sindy Ann!)

Fer de los' ell en yard is a huntin' fer de mornin'
    (Hi O! git 'long! go 'way!)
En she'll ketch up widdus 'fo' we ever git dis corn in.
    (Oh, go 'way Sindy Ann!)

IV

THE PLOUGH-HANDS' SONG

(JASPER COUNTY—1860.)

NIGGER mighty happy w'en he layin' by co'n—
    Dat sun's a slantin';
Nigger mighty happy w'en he year de dinner-ho'n—
    Dat sun's a slantin';
En he mo' happy still w'en de night draws on—
    Dat sun's a slantin';
Dat sun's a slantin' des ez sho's you bo'n!
    En it's rise up, Primus! fetch anudder yell:
    Dat ole dun cow's des a shakin' up 'er bell,
    En de frogs chunin' up 'fo' de jew done fell:
    Good-night, Mr. Killdee! I wish you mighty well!
      —Mr. Killdee! I wish you mighty well!
        —I wish you mighty well!

De co'n 'll be ready 'g'inst dumplin day—
    Dat sun's a slantin';
But nigger gotter watch, en stick, en stay—
    Dat sun's a slantin';
Same ez de bee-martin watchin' un de jay—
    Dat sun's a slantin';
Dat sun's a slantin' en a slippin' away!
    Den it's rise up, Primus! en gin it t'um strong;
    De cow's gwine home wid der ding-dang-dong—

Sling in anudder tetch er de ole-time song:
Good-night, Mr. Whipperwill! don't stay long!
—Mr. Whipperwill! don't stay long!
—Don't stay long!

V

CHRISTMAS PLAY-SONG

(MYRICK PLACE, PUTNAM COUNTY—1858.)

HI my rinktum!   Black gal sweet,
Same like goodies w'at de w'ite folks eat;
Ho my Riley! don't you take'n tell 'er name,
En den ef sumpin' happen you won't ketch de blame;
Hi my rinktum! better take'n hide yo' plum;
Joree don't holler eve'y time he fine a wum.
            Den it's hi my rinktum!
                Don't git no udder man;
                    En it's ho my Riley!
                    Fetch out Miss Dilsey Ann!

Ho my Riley!   Yaller gal fine;
She may be yone but she oughter be mine!
Hi my rinktum!   Lemme git by,
En see w'at she mean by de cut er dat eye!
Ho my Riley! better shet dat do'—
De w'ite folks 'll b'leeve we er t'arin up de flo'.

Den it's ho my Riley!
Come a siftin' up ter me!
En it's hi my rinktum!
Dis de way ter twis' yo' knee!

Hi my rinktum! Ain't de eas' gittin' red?
De squinch owl shiver like he wanter go ter bed;
Ho my Riley! but de gals en de boys,
Des now gittin' so dey kin sorter make a noise.
Hi my rinktum! let de yaller gal 'lone;
Niggers don't hanker arter sody in de pone.
Den it's hi my rinktum!
Better try anudder plan;
An' it's ho my Riley!
Trot out Miss Dilsey Ann!

Ho my Riley! In de happy Chrismus' time
De niggers shake der cloze a huntin' fer a dime.
Hi my rinktum! En den dey shake der feet,
En greaze derse'f wid de good ham meat.
Ho my Riley! dey eat en dey cram,
En bimeby ole Miss 'll be a sendin' out de dram.
Den it's ho my Riley!
You hear dat, Sam!
En it's hi my rinktum!
Be a sendin' out de dram!

VI

PLANTATION PLAY-SONG

(Putnam County—1856.)

Hit's a gittin' mighty late, w'en de Guinny-hins
   squall,
En you better dance now, ef you gwineter dance a
   tall,
Fer by dis time ter-morrer night you can't hardly
   crawl,
Kaze you'll hatter
   take de hoe ag'in
   en likewise de
   maul—
Don't you hear dat
   bay colt a kickin'
   in his stall?
Stop yo' humpin' up
   yo' sho'lders—
      Dat'll never do!
Hop light, ladies,
      Oh, Miss Loo!
      Hit takes a heap er scrougin'
         Fer ter git you thoo—
      Hop light, ladies,
         Oh, Miss Loo!

Ef you niggers don't watch, you'll sing anudder
    chune,
Fer de sun'll rise'n ketch you ef you don't be mighty
    soon;
En de stars is gittin' paler, en de ole gray coon
Is a settin' in de grape-vine a watchin' fer de moon.
    W'en a feller comes a knockin'
       Des holler—*Oh, shoo!*
    Hop light, ladies,
       Oh, Miss Loo!
    Oh, swing dat yaller gal!
       Do, boys, do!
    Hop light, ladies,
       Oh, Miss Loo!

Oh, tu'n me loose! Lemme 'lone! Go way, now!
W'at you speck I come a dancin' fer ef I dunno how?
Deze de ve'y kinder footses w'at kicks up a row;
Can't you jump inter de middle en make yo' gal a
    bow?
    Look at dat merlatter man
       A follerin' up Sue;
    Hop light, ladies,
       Oh, Miss Loo!
    De boys ain't a gwine
       W'en you cry *boo hoo*—
    Hop light, ladies,
       Oh, Miss Loo!

TRANSCRIPTIONS *

1. A PLANTATION CHANT

Hit's eighteen hunder'd forty-en-fo',
Christ done open dat He'v'mly do'—
    An' I don't wanter stay yer no longer;
Hit's eighteen hunder'd forty-en-five,
Christ done made dat dead man alive—
    An' I don't wanter stay yer no longer.
      You ax me ter run home,
        Little childun—
      Run home, dat sun done roll—
    An' I don't wanter stay yer no longer.

Hit's eighteen hunder'd forty-en-six,
Christ is got us a place done fix—
    An' I don't wanter stay yer no longer;
Hit's eighteen hunder'd forty-en-sev'm
Christ done sot a table in Hev'm—
    An' I don't wanter stay yer no longer.

---

* If these are adaptations from songs the negroes have caught from the whites, their origin is very remote. I have transcribed them literally, and I regard them as in the highest degree characteristic.

You ax me ter run home,
　Little childun—
Run home, dat sun done roll—
　An' I don't wanter stay yer no longer.

Hit's eighteen hunder'd forty-en-eight,
Christ done make dat crooked way straight—
　An' I don't wanter stay yer no longer;
Hit's eighteen hunder'd forty-en-nine,
Christ done tu'n dat water inter wine—
　An' I don't wanter stay yer no longer.
　　You ax me ter run home,
　　　Little childun—
　　Run home, dat sun done roll—
　　　An' I don't wanter stay yer no longer.

Hit's eighteen hunder'd forty-en-ten,
Christ is de mo'ner's onliest fr'en'—
　An' I don't wanter stay yer no longer;
Hit's eighteen hunder'd forty-en-'lev'm,
Christ'll be at de do' w'en we all git ter Hev'm—
　An' I don't wanter stay yer no longer.
　　You ax me ter run home,
　　　Little childun—
　　Run home, dat sun done roll—
　　　An' I don't wanter stay yer no longer.

2. A Plantation
Serenade

De ole bee make de honey-
    comb,
  De young bee make de
    honey,
De niggers make de cotton en
    co'n,
  En de w'ite folks gits de
    money.

De raccoon he's a cu'us man,
  He never walk twel dark,
En nuthin' never 'sturbs his mine,
  Twel he hear ole Bringer bark.

    De raccoon totes a bushy tail,
      De 'possum totes no ha'r,
    Mr. Rabbit, he come skippin' by,
      He ain't got none ter spar'.

    Monday mornin' break er day,
      W'ite folks got me gwine,
    But Sat'dy night, w'en de sun goes down,
      Dat yaller gal's in my mine.

    Fifteen poun' er meat a week,
      W'isky fer ter sell,
    Oh, how can a young man stay at home,
      Dem gals dey look so well?

Met a 'possum in de road—
Brer 'Possum, whar you gwine?
I thank my stars, I bless my life,
I'm a huntin' fer de muscadine.

VIII

THE BIG BETHEL CHURCH

De Big Bethel chu'ch! de Big Bethel chu'ch!
  Done put ole Satun behine um;
Ef a sinner git loose fum enny udder chu'ch,
  De Big Bethel chu'ch will fine um!

Hit's good ter be dere, en it's sweet ter be dere,
  Wid de sisterin' all aroun' you—
A shakin' dem shackles er mussy en' love
  Wharwid de Lord is boun' you.

Hit's sweet ter be dere en lissen ter de hymes,
  En hear dem mo'ners a shoutin'—
Dey done reach de place whar der ain't no room
  Fer enny mo' weepin' en doubtin'.

Hit's good ter be dere w'en de sinners all jine
  Wid de brudderin in dere singin',
En it look like Gaberl gwine ter rack up en blow
  En set dem heav'm bells ter ringin'!

Oh, de Big Bethel chu'ch! de Big Bethel chu'ch,
  Done put ole Satun behine um;
Ef a sinner git loose fum enny udder chu'ch
  De Big Bethel chu'ch will fine um!

IX

TIME GOES BY TURNS

DAR's a pow'ful rassle 'twix de Good en de **Bad,**
  En de Bad's got de all-under holt;
En w'en de wuss come, she come i'on-clad,
  En you hatter hole yo' bref fer de jolt.

But des todes de las' Good gits de knee-lock,
  En dey draps ter de groun'—*ker flop!*
Good had de inturn, en he stan' like a rock,
  En he bleedzd fer ter be on top.

De dry wedder breaks wid a big thunder-clap,
  Fer dey ain't no drout' w'at kin las',
But de seasons w'at whoops up de cotton crap,
  Likewise dey freshens up de grass.

De rain fall so saf' in de long dark night,
  Twel you hatter hole yo' han' fer a sign,
But de drizzle w'at sets de tater-slips right
  Is de makin' er de May-pop vine.

In de mellerest groun' de clay root'll ketch
　En hole ter de tongue er de plow,
En a pine-pole gate at de gyardin-patch
　Never'll keep out de ole brindle cow.

One en all on us knows who's a pullin' at de bits
　Like de lead-mule dat g'ides by de rein,
En yit, somehow er nudder, de bestest un us gits
　Mighty sick er de tuggin' at de chain.

Hump yo'se'f ter de load en fergit de distress,
　En dem w'at stan's by ter scoff,
Fer de harder de pullin', de longer de res',
　En de bigger de feed in de troff.

A STORY OF THE WAR

A STORY OF THE WAR

WHEN Miss Theodosia Huntingdon, of Burlington, Vermont, concluded to come South in 1870, she was moved by three considerations. In the first place, her brother, John Huntingdon, had become a citizen of Georgia—having astonished his acquaintances by marrying a young lady, the male members of whose family had achieved considerable distinction in the Confederate army; in the second place, she was anxious to explore a region which she almost unconsciously pictured to herself as remote and semi-

barbarous; and, in the third place, her friends had
persuaded her that to some extent she was an invalid.
It was in vain that she argued with herself as to the
propriety of undertaking the journey alone and un-
protected, and she finally put an end to inward and
outward doubts by informing herself and her friends,
including John Huntingdon, her brother, who was
practicing law in Atlanta, that she had decided to
visit the South.

When, therefore, on the 12th of October, 1870—
the date is duly recorded in one of Miss Theodosia's
letters—she alighted from the cars in Atlanta, in the
midst of a great crowd, she fully expected to find her
brother waiting to receive her. The bells of several
locomotives were ringing, a number of trains were
moving in and out, and the porters and baggage-men
were screaming and bawling to such an extent that
for several moments Miss Huntingdon was consider-
ably confused; so much so that she paused in the
hope that her brother would suddenly appear and
rescue her from the smoke, and dust, and din. At
that moment some one touched her on the arm, and
she heard a strong, half-confident, half-apologetic
voice exclaim:

"Ain't dish yer Miss Doshy?"

Turning, Miss Theodosia saw at her side a tall,
gray-haired negro. Elaborating the incident afterward
to her friends, she was pleased to say that the appear-

ance of the old man was somewhat picturesque. He
stood towering above her, his hat in one hand, a car-
riage-whip in the other, and an expectant smile light-
ing up his rugged face. She remembered a name her
brother had often used in his letters, and, with a
woman's tact, she held out her hand, and said:
"Is this Uncle Remus?"

"Law, Miss Doshy! how you know de ole nigger?
I know'd you by de faver; but how you know me?"
And then, without waiting for a reply: "Miss Sally,
she sick in bed, en Mars John, he bleedzd ter go in de
country, en dey tuck'n sont me. I know'd you de
minnit I laid eyes on you. Time I seed you, I say ter
myse'f, 'I lay dar's Miss Doshy,' en, sho nuff, dar
you wuz. You ain't gun up yo' checks, is you? Kaze
I'll git de trunk sont up by de 'spress waggin."

The next moment Uncle Remus was elbowing his
way unceremoniously through the crowd, and in a
very short time, seated in the carriage driven by the
old man, Miss Huntingdon was whirling through the
streets of Atlanta in the direction of her brother's
home. She took advantage of the opportunity to study
the old negro's face closely, her natural curiosity con-
siderably sharpened by a knowledge of the fact that
Uncle Remus had played an important part in her
brother's history. The result of her observation must
have been satisfactory, for presently she laughed, and
said:

"Uncle Remus, you haven't told me how you knew me in that great crowd."

The old man chuckled, and gave the horses a gentle rap with the whip.

"Who? Me! I know'd you by de faver. Dat boy er Mars John's is de ve'y spit en immij un you. I'd a know'd you in New 'Leens, let 'lone down dar in de kyar-shed."

This was Miss Theodosia's introduction to Uncle Remus. One Sunday afternoon, a few weeks after her arrival, the family were assembled in the piazza enjoying the mild weather. Mr. Huntingdon was reading a newspaper; his wife was crooning softly as she rocked the baby to sleep; and the little boy was endeavoring to show his Aunt Dosia the outlines of Kenesaw Mountain through the purple haze that hung like a wonderfully fashioned curtain in the sky and almost obliterated the horizon. While they were thus engaged, Uncle Remus came around the corner of the house, talking to himself.

"Dey er too lazy ter wuk," he was saying, "en dey specks hones' fokes fer ter stan' up en s'port um. I'm gwine down ter Putmon County whar Mars Jeems is —dat's w'at I'm agwine ter do."

"What's the matter now, Uncle Remus?" inquired Mr. Huntingdon, folding up his newspaper.

"Nuthin' 'tall, Mars John, 'ceppin deze yer sunshine niggers. Dey begs my terbacker, en borrys my

tools, en steals my vittles, en hit's done come ter dat
pass dat I gotter pack up en go. I'm agwine down ter
Putmon, dat's w'at."

Uncle Remus was accustomed to make this threat
several times a day, but upon this occasion it seemed
to remind Mr. Huntingdon of something.

"Very well," he said, "I'll come around and help
you pack up, but before you go I want you to tell
Sister here how you went to war and fought for the
Union.—Remus was a famous warrior," he continued,
turning to Miss Theodosia; "he volunteered for one
day, and commanded an army of one. You know the
story, but you have never heard Remus's version."

Uncle Remus shuffled around in an awkward, embarrassed way, scratched his head, and looked un-
comfortable.

"Miss Doshy ain't got no time fer ter set dar an
year de ole nigger run on."

"Oh, yes, I have, Uncle Remus!" exclaimed the
young lady; "plenty of time."

The upshot of it was that, after many ridiculous
protests, Uncle Remus sat down on the steps, and
proceeded to tell his story of the war. Miss Theodosia
listened with great interest, but throughout it all she
observed—and she was painfully conscious of the fact,
as she afterward admitted—that Uncle Remus spoke
from the standpoint of a Southerner, and with the air

of one who expected his hearers to thoroughly sympathize with him.

"Co'se," said Uncle Remus, addressing himself to Miss Theodosia, "you ain't bin to Putmon, en you dunner whar de Brad Slaughter place en Harmony Grove is, but Mars John en Miss Sally, dey bin dar a time er two, en dey knows how de lan' lays. Well, den, it 'uz right 'long in dere whar Mars Jeems lived, en whar he live now. When de war come 'long he wuz livin' dere longer Ole Miss en Miss Sally. Ole Miss 'uz his ma, en Miss Sally dar 'uz his sister. De war come des like I tell you, en marters sorter rock along same like dey allers did. Hit didn't strike me dat dey wuz enny war gwine on, en ef I hadn't sorter miss de nabers, en seed fokes gwine outer de way fer ter ax de news, I'd a 'lowed ter myse'f dat de war wuz 'way off 'mong some yuther country. But all dis time de fuss wuz gwine on, en Mars Jeems, he wuz des eatchin' fer ter put in. Ole Miss en Miss Sally, dey tuck on so he didn't git off de fus' year, but bimeby news come down dat times wuz gittin' putty hot, en Mars Jeems he got up, he did, en say he gotter go, en go he did. He got a overseer fer ter look atter de place, en he went en jined de army. En he 'uz a fighter, too, mon, Mars Jeems wuz. Many's en many's de time," continued the old man, reflectively, "dat I hatter take'n bresh dat boy on accounter his 'buzin' en beatin' dem yuther boys. He went off dar fer ter

fight, en he fit. Ole Miss useter call me up Sunday
en read w'at de papers say 'bout Mars Jeems, en it
hope 'er up might'ly. I kin see 'er des like it 'uz
yistiddy.

"'Remus,' sez she, 'dish yer's w'at de papers say
'bout my baby,' en den she'd read out twel she
couldn't read fer cryin'. Hit went on dis way year in
en year out, en dem wuz lonesome times, sho's you
bawn, Miss Doshy—lonesome times, sho. Hit got
hotter en hotter in de war, en lonesomer en mo' lonesomer at home, en bimeby 'long come de conscrip'
man, en he des everlas'nly scoop up Mars Jeems's
overseer. W'en dis come 'bout, ole Miss, she sont
atter me en say, sez she:

"'Remus, I ain't got nobody fer ter look arter de
place but you,' sez she, en den I up'n say, sez I:

"'Mistiss, you kin des 'pen' on de ole nigger.'

"I wuz ole den, Miss Doshy—let 'lone w'at I is
now; en you better b'leeve I bossed dem han's. I had
dem niggers up en in de fiel' long 'fo' day, en de way
dey did wuk wuz a caution. Ef dey didn't earnt der
vittles dat season den I ain't name Remus. But dey
wuz tuk keer un. Dey had plenty er cloze en plenty
er grub, en dey wuz de fattes' niggers in de settlement.

"Bimeby one day, Ole Miss, she call me up en say
de Yankees done gone en tuck Atlanty—dish yer ve'y
town; den present'y I year dey wuz a marchin' on

down todes Putmon, en, lo en beholes! one day, de
fus news I know'd, Mars Jeems he rid up wid a whole
gang er men. He des stop long nuff fer ter change
hosses en snatch a mouffle er sump'n ter eat, but 'fo'
he rid off, he call me up en say, sez he:

"'Daddy'—all Ole Miss's chilluns call me daddy
—'Daddy,' he say, ''pears like dere's gwineter be
mighty rough times 'roun' yer. De Yankees, dey er
done got ter Madison en Mounticellar, en 'twon't be
many days 'fo' dey er down yer. 'Tain't likely dey'll
pester mother ner sister; but, daddy, ef de wus come
ter de wus, I speck you ter take keer un um,' sezee.

"Den I say, sez I: 'How long you bin knowin'
me, Mars Jeems?' sez I.

"'Sence I wuz a baby,' sezee.

"'Well, den, Mars Jeems,' sez I, 'you know'd
'twa'nt no use fer ter ax me ter take keer Ole Miss en
Miss Sally.'

"Den he tuck'n squoze my han' en jump on de
filly I bin savin' fer 'im, en rid off. One time he tu'n
'roun' en look like he wanter say sump'n', but he des
waf' his han'—so—en gallop on. I know'd den dat
trouble wuz brewin'. Nigger dat knows he's gwineter
git thumped kin sorter fix hisse'f, en I tuck'n fix up
like de war wuz gwineter come right in at de front
gate. I tuck'n got all de cattle en hosses tergedder en
driv' um ter de fo'-mile place, en I tuck all de corn en
fodder en w'eat, en put um in a crib out dar in de

woods; en I bilt me a pen in de swamp, en dar I put
de hogs. Den, w'en I fix all dis, I put on my Sunday
cloze en groun' my axe. Two whole days I groun' dat
axe. De grinestone wuz in sight er de gate en close
ter de big 'ouse, en dar I tuck my stan'.

"Bimeby one day, yer come de Yankees. Two un
um come fus, en den de whole face er de yeath
swawm'd wid um. De fus glimpse I kotch un um,
I tuck my axe en march inter Ole Miss settin'-room.
She done had de sidebode move in dar, en I wish I
may drap ef 'twuzn't fa'rly blazin' wid silver—silver
cups en silver sassers, silver plates en silver dishes,
silver mugs en silver pitchers. Look like ter me dey
wuz fixin' fer a weddin'. Dar sot Ole Miss des ez
prim en ez proud ez ef she own de whole county.
Dis kinder hope me up, kaze I done seed Ole Miss
look dat away once befo' w'en de overseer struck me
in de face wid a w'ip. I sot down by de fier wid my
axe 'tween my knees. Dar we sot w'iles de Yankees
ransack de place. Miss Sally, dar, she got sorter rest-
less, but Ole Miss didn't skasely bat 'er eyes. Bimeby,
we hear steps on de peazzer, en yer come a couple
er young fellers wid strops on der shoulders, en der
sodes a draggin' on de flo', en der spurrers a rattlin'.
I won't say I wuz skeer'd," said Uncle Remus, as
though endeavoring to recall something he failed to
remember, "I won't say I wuz skeer'd, kaze I wuzent; but I wuz took'n wid a mighty funny feelin'

in de naberhood er de gizzard. Dey wuz mighty perlite, dem young chaps wuz; but Ole Miss, she never tu'n 'er head, en Miss Sally, she look straight at de fier. Bimeby one un um see me, en he say, sezee:

" 'Hello, ole man, w'at you doin' in yer?' sezee.

" 'Well, boss,' sez I, 'I bin cuttin' some wood fer Ole Miss, en I des stop fer ter wom my han's a little,' sez I.

" 'Hit is cole, dat's a fack,' sezee.

"Wid dat I got up en tuck my stan' behime Ole Miss en Miss Sally, en de man w'at speak, he went up en wom his han's. Fus thing you know, he raise up sudden, en say, sezee:

" 'W'at dat on yo' axe?'

" 'Dat's de fier shinin' on it,' sez I.

" 'Hit look like blood,' sezee, en den he laft.

"But, bless yo' soul, dat man wouldn't never laft dat day ef he'd know'd de wukkins er Remus's mine. But dey didn't bodder nobody ner tech nuthin', en bimeby dey put out. Well, de Yankees, dey kep' passin' all de mawnin' en it look like ter me dey wuz a string un um ten mile long. Den dey commence gittin' thinner en thinner, en den atter w'ile we hear skummishin' in de naberhood er Armer's fe'y, en Ole Miss 'low how dat wuz Wheeler's men makin' persoot. Mars Jeems wuz wid dem Wheeler fellers, en I know'd ef dey wuz dat close I wa'n't doin' no good settin' 'roun' de house toas'n my shins at de fier, so I des tuck Mars Jeems's rifle fum behine de do' en put out ter look atter my stock.

"Seem like I ain t never see no raw day like dat, needer befo' ner since. Dey wa'n't no rain, but de wet des sifted down; mighty raw day. De leaves on de groun' 'uz so wet dey don't make no fuss, en I got in de woods, en w'enever I year de Yankees gwine by, I des stop in my tracks en let un pass. I wuz stan'in' dat away in de aidge er de woods lookin' out 'cross a clearin', w'en—*piff!*—out come a little bunch er blue smoke fum de top er wunner dem big lonesome-lookin' pines, en den—*pow!*

"Sez I ter myse'f, sez I: 'Honey, youer right on my route, en I'll des see w'at kinder bird you got roostin' in you,' en w'iles I wuz a lookin' out bus' de smoke—*piff!* en den—*bang!* Wid dat I des drapt back inter de woods, en sorter skeerted 'roun' so's ter git de tree 'twixt' me en de road. I slid up putty close, en wadder you speck I see? Des ez sho's youer settin' dar lissenin' dey wuz a live Yankee up dar in dat tree, en he wuz a loadin' en a shootin' at de boys dez ez cool es a cowcumber in de jew, en he had his hoss hitch out in de bushes, kaze I year de creetur tromplin' 'roun'. He had a spy-glass up dar, en w'iles I wuz a watchin' un 'im, he raise 'er up en look thoo 'er, en den he lay er down en fix his gun fer ter shoot. I had good eyes in dem days, ef I ain't got um now, en 'way up de big road I see Mars Jeems a comin'. Hit wuz too fur fer ter see his face, but I know'd 'im by de filly w'at I raise fer 'im, en she wuz a prancin' like a school-gal. I know'd dat man wuz gwineter shoot Mars Jeems ef he could, en dat wuz mo'n I could stan'. Manys en manys de time dat I nuss dat boy, en hilt 'im in dese arms, en toted 'im on dis back, en w'en I see dat Yankee lay dat gun 'cross a lim' en take aim at Mars Jeems I up wid my ole rifle, en shet my eyes en let de man have all she had."

"Do you mean to say," exclaimed Miss Theodosia, indignantly, "that you shot the Union soldier, when you knew he was fighting for your freedom?"

"Co'se, I know all about dat," responded Uncle Remus, "en it sorter made cole chills run up my back; but w'en I see dat man take aim, en Mars Jeems gwine home ter Ole Miss en Miss Sally, I des disremembered all 'bout freedom en lammed aloose. En den atter dat, me en Miss Sally tuck en nuss de man right straight along. He los' one arm in dat tree bizness, but me en Miss Sally we nuss 'im en we nuss 'im twel he done got well. Des 'bout dat time I quit nuss'n 'im, but Miss Sally she kep' on. She kep' on," continued Uncle Remus, pointing to Mr. Huntingdon, "en now dar he is."

"But you cost him an arm," exclaimed Miss Theodosia.

"I gin 'im dem," said Uncle Remus, pointing to Mrs. Huntingdon, "en I gin 'im deze"—holding up his own brawny arms. "En ef dem ain't nuff fer enny man den I done los' de way."

HIS SAYINGS

JEEMS ROBER'SON'S LAST ILLNESS

A JONESBORO negro, while waiting for the train to go out, met up with Uncle Remus. After the usual "time of day" had been passed between the two, the former inquired about an acquaintance.

"How's Jeems Rober'son?" he asked.

"Ain't you year 'bout Jim?" asked Uncle Remus.

"Dat I ain't," responded the other; "I ain't hear talk er Jem sence he cut loose fum de chain-gang. Dat w'at make I ax. He ain't down wid de biliousness, is he?"

"Not dat I knows un," responded Uncle Remus, gravely. "He ain't sick, an' he ain't bin sick. He des tuck'n say he wuz gwineter ride dat ar roan mule er Mars John's de udder Sunday, an' de mule, she up'n do

219

like she got nudder ingagement. I done bin fool wid
dat mule befo', an' I tuck'n tole Jim dat he better not
git tangle up wid 'er; but Jim, he up'n 'low dat he
wuz a hoss-doctor, an' wid dat he ax me fer a chaw
terbarker, en den he got de bridle, en tuck'n kotch
de mule en got on her— Well," continued Uncle
Remus, looking uneasily around, "I speck you better
go git yo' ticket. Dey tells me dish yer train goes a
callyhootin'."

"Hole on dar, Uncle Remus; you ain't tell me 'bout
Jim," exclaimed the Jonesboro negro.

"I done tell you all I knows, chile. Jim, he tuck'n
light on de mule, an' de mule she up'n hump 'erse'f,
an den dey wuz a skuffle, an' w'en de dus' blow 'way,
dar lay de nigger on de groun', an' de mule she stood
eatin' at de troff wid wunner Jim's gallusses wrop
'roun' her behime-leg. Den atterwuds, de ker'ner, he
come 'roun', an' he tuck'n gin it out dat Jim died
sorter accidental like. Hit's des like I tell you: de
nigger wern't sick a minnit. So long! Bimeby you
won't ketch yo' train. I got ter be knockin' long."

II

UNCLE REMUS'S CHURCH EXPERIENCE

THE deacon of a colored church met Uncle Remus
recently, and, after some uninteresting remarks about
the weather, asked:

"How dis you don't come down ter chu'ch no mo', Brer Remus? We er bin er havin' some mighty 'freshen' times lately."

"Hit's bin a long time sence I bin down dar, Brer Rastus, an' hit'll be longer. I done got my dose."

"You ain't done gone an' unjined, is you, Brer Remus?"

"Not zackly, Brer Rastus. I des tuck'n draw'd out. De members 'uz a blame sight too mutuel fer ter suit my doctrines."

"How wuz dat, Brer Remus?"

"Well, I tell you, Brer Rastus. W'en I went ter dat chu'ch, I went des ez umbill ez de nex' one. I went dar fer ter sing, an' fer ter pray, an' fer ter wushup, an' I mos' giner'lly allers had a stray shin-plarster w'ich de ole 'oman say she want sont out dar ter dem cullud fokes 'cross de water. Hit went on dis way twel bimeby, one day, de fus news I know'd der was a row got up in de amen cornder. Brer Dick, he 'nounced dat dey wern't nuff money in de box; an' Brer Sim said if dey wern't he speck Brer Dick know'd whar it disappeared ter; an' den Brer Dick 'low'd dat he won't stan' no 'probusness, an' wid dat he haul off an' tuck Brer Sim under de jaw—*ker blap!* —an' den dey clinched an' drapped on de flo' an' fout under de benches an' 'mong de wimmen.

" 'Bout dat time Sis Tempy, she lipt up in de a'r, an' sing out dat she done gone an tromple on de Ole

Boy, an' she kep' on lippin' up an' slingin' out 'er han's twel bimeby—*blip!*—she tuck Sis Becky in de mouf, an' den Sis Becky riz an' fetch a grab at Sis Tempy, an' I 'clar' ter grashus ef didn't 'pear ter me like she got a poun' er wool. Atter dat de revivin' sorter het up like. Bofe un um had kin 'mong de mo'ners, an' ef you ever see skufflin' an' scramblin' hit wuz den an' dar. Brer Jeems Henry, he mounted Brer Plato an' rid 'im over de railin', an' den de preacher he start down fum de pulpit, an' des ez he wuz skippin' onter de flatform a hyme-book kotch 'im in de bur er de year, an' I be bless ef it didn't soun' like a bung-shell'd busted. Des den, Brer Jesse, he riz up in his seat, sorter keerless like, an' went down inter his britches atter his razer, an' right den I know'd sho' nuff trubble wuz begun. Sis Dilsey, she seed it herse'f, an' she tuck'n let off wunner dem hallyluyah hollers, an' den I disremember w'at come ter pass.

"I'm gittin' sorter ole, Brer Rastus, an' it seem like de dus' sorter shet out de pannyrammer. Fuddermo', my lim's got ter akin, mo' speshully w'en I year Brer

Sim an' Brer Dick a snortin' and a skufflin' under de benches like ez dey wuz sorter makin' der way ter my pew. So I kinder hump myse'f an' scramble out, and de fus man w'at I seed was a p'leeceman, an' he had a nigger 'rested, an' de fergiven name er dat nigger wuz Remus."

"He didn't 'res' you, did he, Brer Remus?"

"Hit's des like I tell you, Brer Rastus, an' I hatter git Mars John fer to go inter my bon's fer me. Hit ain't no use fer ter sing out chu'ch ter me, Brer Rastus. I done bin an' got my dose. W'en I goes ter war, I wanter know w'at I'm a doin'. I don't wanter git hemmed up 'mong no wimmen and preachers. I wants elbow-room, an' I'm bleedzd ter have it. Des gimme elbow-room."

"But, Brer Remus, you ain't—"

"I mout drap in, Brer Rastus, an' den ag'in I moutn't, but w'en you duz see me santer in de do', wid my specs on, youk'n des say to de congergashun, sorter familious like, 'Yer come ole man Remus wid his hoss-pistol, an' ef dar's much uv a skuffle 'roun' yer dis evenin' youer gwineter year fum 'im.' Dat's me, an' dat's what you kin tell um. So long! Member me to Sis Abby."

III

UNCLE REMUS AND THE SAVANNAH DARKEY

THE notable difference existing between the negroes in the interior of the cotton States and those on the seaboard—a difference that extends to habits and opinions as well as to dialect—has given rise to certain ineradicable prejudices which are quick to display themselves whenever an opportunity offers. These prejudices were forcibly, as well as ludicrously, illustrated in Atlanta recently. A gentleman from Savannah had been spending the summer in the mountains of north Georgia, and found it convenient to take along a body-servant. This body-servant was a very fine specimen of the average coast negro—sleek, well-conditioned, and consequential—disposed to regard with undisguised contempt everything and everybody not indigenous to the rice-growing region—and he paraded around the streets with quite a curious and critical air. Espying Uncle Remus languidly sunning himself on a corner, the Savannah darkey approached.

"Mornin', sah."

"I'm sorter up an' about," responded Uncle Remus, carelessly and calmly. "How is you stannin' it?"

"Tanky you, my helt mos' so-so. He mo' hot dun in de mountain. Seem so lak man mus' git need *

---

* Underneath.

de shade. I enty fer see no rice-bud in dis
pa'ts."

"In dis w'ich?" inquired Uncle Remus, with a
sudden affectation of interest.

"In dis pa'ts. In dis country.
Da plenty in Sawanny."

"Plenty whar?"

"Da plenty in Sawanny. I
enty fer see no crab an' no
oscher; en swimp, he no stay
'roun'. I lak some rice-bud
now."

"Youer talkin' 'bout deze
yer sparrers, w'ich dey er all
head, en 'lev'm un makes one
mouffle,* I speck," suggested Uncle Remus. "Well,
dey er yer," he continued, "but dis ain't no climate
whar de rice-birds flies inter yo' pockets en gits out
de money an' makes de change derse'f; an' de isters
don't shuck off der shells en run over you on de
street, an' no mo' duz de s'imp hull derse'f an' drap
in yo' mouf. But dey er yer, dough. De scads 'll
fetch um."

"Him po' country fer true," commented the Savannah negro; "he no like Sawanny. Down da, we
set need de shade an' eaty de rice-bud, an' de crab, an'
de swimp tree time de day; an' de buckra man drinky

---

* Mouthful.

him wine, an' smoky him seegyar all troo de night. Plenty fer eat an' not much fer wuk."

"Hit's mighty nice, I speck," responded Uncle Remus, gravely. "De nigger dat ain't hope up 'longer high feedin' ain't got no grip. But up yer whar fokes is gotter scramble 'roun' an' make der own livin', de vittles wat's kumerlated widout enny sweatin' mos' allers gener'lly b'longs ter some yuther man by rights. One hoe-cake an' a rasher er middlin' meat las's me fum Sunday ter Sunday, an' I'm in a mighty big streak er luck w'en I gits dat."

The Savannah negro here gave utterance to a loud, contemptuous laugh, and began to fumble somewhat ostentatiously with a big brass watch-chain.

"But I speck I struck up wid a payin' job las' Chuseday," continued Uncle Remus, in a hopeful tone.

"Wey you gwan do?"

"Oh, I'm a waitin' on a culled gemmun fum Savannah—wunner deze yer high livers you bin tellin' 'bout."

"How dat?"

"I loant 'im two dollars," responded Uncle Remus, grimly, "an' I'm a waitin' on 'im fer de money. Hit's wunner deze yer jobs w'at las's a long time."

The Savannah negro went off after his rice-birds, while Uncle Remus leaned up against the wall and laughed until he was in imminent danger of falling down from sheer exhaustion.

IV.

TURNIP SALAD AS A TEXT

As Uncle Remus was going down the street recently he was accosted by several acquaintances.

"Heyo!" said one, "here comes Uncle Remus. He look like he gwine fer ter set up a bo'din-house."

Several others bantered the old man, but he appeared to be in a good humor. He was carrying a huge basket of vegetables.

"How many er you boys," said he, as he put his basket down, "is done a han's turn dis day? En yit de week's done commence. I year talk er niggers dat's got money in de bank, but I lay hit ain't none er you fellers. Whar you speck you gwineter git yo' dinner, en how you speck you gwineter git 'long?"

"Oh, we sorter knocks 'roun' an' picks up a livin'," responded one.

"Dat's w'at make I say w'at I duz," said Uncle Remus. "Fokes go 'bout in de day-time an' makes a livin', an' you come 'long w'en dey er res'in' der bones

an' picks it up. I ain't no han' at figgers, but I lay I
k'n count up right yer in de san' en number up how
menny days hit'll be 'fo' you'er cuppled on ter de
chain-gang."

"De ole man's holler'n now sho'," said one of the
listeners, gazing with admiration on the venerable
old darkey.

"I ain't takin' no chances 'bout vittles. Hit's
proned inter me fum de fus dat I got ter eat, en I
knows dat I got fer ter grub for w'at I gits. Hit's
agin de mor'l law fer niggers fer ter eat w'en dey
don't wuk, an' w'en you see um 'pariently fattenin' on
a'r, you k'n des bet dat ruinashun's gwine on some'rs.
I got mustard, en poke salid, en lam's quarter in dat
baskit, en me en my ole 'oman gwineter sample it. Ef
enny you boys git a invite you come, but ef you don't
you better stay 'way. I gotter muskit out dar w'at's
used ter persidin' 'roun' whar dey's a cripple nigger.
Don't you fergit dat off'n yo' mine."

V

A CONFESSION

"W'at's dis yer I see, great big niggers gwine
'lopin' 'roun' town wid cakes 'n pies fer ter sell?"
asked Uncle Remus recently, in his most scornful
tone.

"That's what they are doing," responded a young man; "that's the way they make a living."

"Dat w'at make I say w'at I duz—dat w'at keep me grum'lin' w'en I goes in cullud fokes s'ciety. Some niggers ain't gwine ter wuk nohow, an' hit's flingin' 'way time fer ter set enny chain-gang traps fer ter ketch um."

"Well, now, here!" exclaimed the young man, in a dramatic tone, "what are you giving us now? Isn't it just as honest and just as regular to sell pies as it is to do any other kind of work?"

"'Tain't dat, boss," said the old man, seeing that he was about to be cornered; "'tain't dat. Hit's de nas'ness un it w'at gits me."

"Oh, get out!"

"Dat's me, boss, up an' down. Ef dere's ruinashun ennywhar in de known wurril, she goes in de comp'ny uv a hongry nigger w'at's a totin' pies 'roun.' Sometimes w'en I git kotch wid empti- ness in de pit er de stum- muck, an' git ter fairly honin' arter sumpin' w'at got substance in it, den hit look like unto me dat I kin stan' flat-footed an' make more cle'r money eatin' pies dan I could if I wuz ter sell

de las' one 'twixt dis an' Chrismus. An' de nigger w'at
k'n trapes 'round wid pies and not git in no alley-way
an' sample um, den I'm bleedzd ter say dat nigger
out-niggers me an' my fambly. So dar now!"

VI

UNCLE REMUS WITH THE TOOTHACHE

WHEN Uncle Remus put in an appearance one
morning recently, his friends knew he had been in
trouble. He had a red cotton handkerchief tied under
his chin, and the genial humor that usually makes his
aged face its dwelling-place had given way to an expression of grim melancholy. The young men about
the office were inclined to chaff him, but his look of
sullen resignation remained unchanged.

"What revival did you attend last night?" inquired
one.

"What was the color of the mule that did the ham-
mering?" asked another.

"I always told the old man that a suburban chicken
coop would fall on him," remarked some one.

"A strange pig has been squealing in his ear," sug·
gested some one else.

But Uncle Remus remained impassive. He seemed
to have lost all interest in what was going on around
him, and he sighed heavily as he seated himself on the

edge of the trash-box in front of the office. Finally some one asked, in a sympathetic tone:

"What is the matter, old man? You look like you'd been through the mill."

"Now you'er knockin' at de back do' sho'. Ef I ain't bin thoo de mill sence day 'fo' yis- tiddy, den dey ain't no mills in de lan'. Ef wunner deze yer scurshun trains had runned over me I couldn't er bin wuss off. I bin trompin' 'roun' in de low- groun's now gwine on seventy-fi' year, but I ain't see no sich times ez dat w'at I done spe'unst now. Boss, is enny er you all ever rastled wid de toofache?"

"Oh, hundreds of times! The toothache isn't any-thing."

"Den you des played 'roun' de aidges. You ain't had de kine w'at kotch me on de underjaw. You mout a had a gum-bile, but you ain't bin boddered wid de toofache. I wuz settin' up talkin' wid my ole 'oman, kinder puzzlin' 'roun' fer ter see whar de nex' meal's vittles wuz a gwineter cum fum, an' I feel a little ache sorter crawlin' 'long on my jaw-bone, kinder feelin' his way. But de ache don't stay long. He sorter hankered 'roun' like, en den crope back whar he come fum. Bimeby I feel 'im comin' agin, an' dis time hit look like he come up closer—kinder skummishin' 'roun' fer ter see how de lan' lay. Den he went off. Present'y I feel 'im comin', an' dis time hit look like he kyar'd de news unto Mary, fer hit feel like der wuz anudder wun wid 'im. Dey crep' up an' crep' 'roun', an' den dey crope off. Bimeby dey come back, an' dis time dey come like dey wuzent 'fear'd er de s'roundin's, fer dey trot right up unto de toof, sorter zamine it like, an' den trot all roun' it, like deze yer circuous hosses. I sot dar mighty ca'm, but I spected dat sump'n' wuz gwine ter happ'n."

"And it happened, did it?" asked some one in the group surrounding the old man.

"Boss, don't you fergit it," responded Uncle Remus, fervidly. "W'en dem aches gallop back dey galloped fer ter stay, an' dey wuz so mixed up dat I couldn't tell one fum de udder. All night long dey racked an' dey galloped, an' w'en dey got tired er rackin' an' gallopin', dey all close in on de ole toof an' thumped it an' gouged at it twel it 'peared unto me dat dey had got de jaw-bone loosened up, an' wuz tryin' fer ter fetch it up thoo de top er my head an' out at der back er my neck. An' dey got wuss nex' day. Mars John, he seed I wuz 'stracted, an' he tole me fer ter

go roun' yere an' git sump'n' put on it, an' de drug
man he 'lowed dat I better have 'er draw'd, an' his
wuds wuzent more'n cole 'fo' wunner deze yer watch-
youmaycollums—wunner deze dentis' mens—had
retched fer it wid a pa'r er tongs w'at don't tu'n loose
w'en dey ketches a holt. Leas'ways dey didn't wid me.
You oughter seed dat toof, boss. Hit wuz wunner
deze yer fo'-prong fellers. Ef she'd a grow'd wrong
eend out'ard, I'd a bin a bad nigger long arter I
jin'd de chu'ch. You year'd my ho'n!"

VII

THE PHONOGRAPH

"Unc Remus," asked a tall, awkward-looking
negro, who was one of a crowd surrounding the old
man, "w'at's dish 'ere w'at dey calls de fonygraf—
dish yer inst'ument w'at kin holler 'roun' like little
chillun in de back yard?"

"I ain't seed um," said Uncle Remus, feeling in
his pocket for a fresh chew of tobacco. "I ain't seed
um, but I year talk un um. Miss Sally wuz a readin'
in de papers las' Chuseday, an' she say dat's it's a
mighty big watchyoumaycollum."

"A mighty big w'ich?" asked one of the crowd.

"A mighty big w'atzisname," answered Uncle Remus, cautiously. "I wuzent up dar close to whar Miss

Sarah wuz a readin', but I kinder geddered in dat it wuz one er deze 'ere w'atzisnames w'at you hollers inter one year an' it comes out er de ud- der. Hit's mighty funny unter me how dese fokes kin go an' prognosticate der ec-koes inter one er deze yer i'on boxes, an' dar hit'll stay on twel de man comes 'long an' tu'ns de handle an' let's de fuss come pilin' out. Bimeby dey'll git ter makin' sho' nuff fokes, an' den dere'll be a racket 'roun' here. Dey tells me dat it goes off like one er deze yer torpedoes."

"You year dat, don't you?" said one or two of the younger negroes.

"Dat's w'at dey tells me," continued Uncle Remus. "Dat's w'at dey sez. Hit's one er deze yer kinder w'atzisnames w'at sasses back w'en you hollers at it."

"W'at dey fix um fer, den?" asked one of the practical negroes.

"Dat's w'at I wanter know," said Uncle Remus, contemplatively. "But dat's w'at Miss Sally wuz a readin' in de paper. All you gotter do is ter holler at de box, an' dar's yo' remarks. Dey goes in, an' dar dey er tooken and dar dey hangs on twel you shakes de box, an' den dey draps out des ez fresh ez deze yer fishes w'at you git fum Savannah, an' you ain't got time fer ter look at dere gills, nudder."

VIII

RACE IMPROVEMENT

"Dere's a kind er limberness 'bout niggers dese days dat's mighty cu'us," remarked Uncle Remus yesterday, as he deposited a pitcher of fresh water upon the exchange table. "I notisses it in de alley-ways an' on de street-cornders. Dey er rackin' up, mon, deze yer cullud fokes is."

"What are you trying to give us now?" inquired one of the young men, in a bilious tone.

"The old man's mind is wandering," said the society editor, smoothing the wrinkles out of his lavender kids.

Uncle Remus laughed. "I speck I is a gittin' mo frailer dan I wuz 'fo' de fahmin days wuz over, but I sees wid my eyes an' I years wid my year, same ez enny er dese yer young bucks w'at goes a gallopin' 'roun' huntin' up devilment, an' w'en I sees de limberness er dese yer cullud people, an' w'en I sees how dey er dancin' up, den I gits sorter hopeful. Dey er kinder ketchin' up wid me."

"How is that?"

"Oh, dey er movin'," responded Uncle Remus.
"Dey er sorter comin' 'roun'. Dey er gittin' so dey

b'leeve dat dey ain't no better dan
de w'ite fokes. W'en freedom come
out de niggers sorter got dere
humps up, an' dey staid dat way,
twel bimeby dey begun fer ter git
hongry, an' den dey begun fer ter
drap inter line right smartually; an'
now," continued the old man, em-
phatically, "dey er des ez palaver-
ous ez dey wuz befo'. de war. Dey
er gittin' on solid groun', mon."

"You think they are improving,
then?"

"Youer chawin' guv'nment now, boss. You slap
de law onter a nigger a time er two, an' larn 'im dat
he's got fer to look atter his own rashuns an' keep
out'n udder fokes's chick'n-coops, an' sorter coax 'im
inter de idee dat he's got ter feed 'is own chilluns, an'
I be blessed ef you ain't got 'im on risin' groun'. An',
mo'n dat, w'en he gits holt er de fack dat a nigger k'n
have yaller fever same ez w'ite folks, you done got
'im on de mo'ners' bench, an' den ef you come down
strong on de p'int dat he oughter stan' fas' by de
fokes w'at hope him w'en he wuz in trouble de job's
done. W'en you does dat, ef you ain't got yo' han's
on a new-made nigger, den my name ain't Remus,

an' ef dat name's bin changed I ain't seen her abbertized."

IX

IN THE RÔLE OF A TARTAR

A CHARLESTON negro who was in Atlanta on the Fourth of July made a mistake. He saw Uncle Remus edging his way through the crowd, and thought he knew him.

"Howdy, Daddy Ben?" the stranger exclaimed. "I tink I nubber see you no mo'. Wey you gwan? He hot fer true, ain't he?"

"Daddy who?" asked Uncle Remus, straightening himself up with dignity. "W'ich?"

"I know you in Charl'son, an' den in Sewanny. I spec I dun grow away from 'membrance."

"You knowed me in Charlstun, and den in Savanny?"

"He been long time, ain't he, Daddy Ben?"

"Dat's w'at's a pesterin' un me. How much you reckon you know'd me?"

"He good while pas'; when I wer' pickaninny. He long time ago. Wey you gwan, Daddy Ben?"

"W'at does you season your recollection wid fer ter make it hole on so?" inquired the old man.

"I dunno. He stick hese'f. I see you comin' 'long 'n I say 'Dey Daddy Ben.' I tink I see you no mo',

an' I shaky you by de han'. Wey you gwan? Dey **no**
place yer wey we git wine?"

Uncle Remus stared at the strange darkey curiously for a moment, and then he seized him by the
arm.

"Come yer, son, whar dey ain't no folks an' lemme

drap some Jawjy 'intment in dem years er yone.
Youer mighty fur ways fum home, an' you wanter be
a lookin' out fer yo'se'f. Fus and fo'mus, youer
thumpin' de wrong watermillion. Youer w'isslin' up
de wrong chube. I ain't tromped roun' de country
much. I ain't bin to Charlstun an' needer is I tuck in
Savanny; but you couldn't rig up no game on me
dat I wouldn't tumble on to it de minit I laid my
eyeballs on you. W'en hit come to dat I'm ole man
Tumbler, fum Tumblersville—I is dat. Hit takes one
er deze yer full-blooded w'ite men fur ter trap my

jedgment. But w'en a nigger comes a jabberin' 'roun'
like he got a mouf full er rice straw, he ain't got no
mo' chance 'long side er me dan a sick sparrer wid a
squinch-owl. You gotter travel wid a circus 'fo' you
gits away wid me. You better go 'long an' git yo'
kyarpet-sack and skip de town. Youer de freshest
nigger w'at I seen yit."

The Charleston negro passed on just as a policeman came up.

"Boss, you see dat smart Ellick?"

"Yes, what's the matter with him?"

"He's one er deze yer scurshun niggers from Charlstun. I seed you a stannin' over agin de cornder yander, an' ef dat nigger'd a drawd his monty kyards on
me, I wuz a gwineter holler fer you. Would youer
come, boss?"

"Why, certainly, Uncle Remus."

"Dat's w'at I 'lowd. Little more'n he'd a bin aboard
er de wrong waggin. Dat's w'at he'd a bin."

x

A CASE OF MEASLES

"You've been looking like you were rather under
the weather for the past week or two, Uncle Remus,"
said a gentleman to the old man.

"You'd be sorter puny, too, boss, if you'der bin
whar I bin."

"Where have you been?"

" 'Pear ter me like ev'eybody done year 'bout dat. Dey ain't no ole nigger my age an' size dat's had no rattliner time dan I is."

"A kind of picnic?"

"Go 'long, boss! w'at you speck I be doin' sailin' 'roun' ter dese yer cullud picnics? Much mo' an' I wouldn't make bread by wukkin fer't, let 'lone fol- lerin' up a passel er boys an' gals all over keration. Boss, ain't you year 'bout it, sho' 'nuff?"

"I haven't, really. What was the matter?"

"I got strucken wid a sickness, an' she hit de ole nigger a joe-darter 'fo' she tu'n 'im loose."

"What kind of sickness?"

"Hit look sorter cu'ous, boss, but ole an' steddy ez I is, I tuck'n kotch de meezles."

"Oh, get out! You are trying to get up a sensation."

"Hit's a natal fack, boss, I declar' ter grashus ef 'tain't. Dey sorter come on wid a cole, like—leas'ways dat's how I commence fer ter suffer, an' den er koff got straddle er de cole—one dese yer koffs w'at look like hit goes ter de foundash'n. I kep' on linger'n' 'roun' sorter keepin' one eye on the rheumatiz an' de udder on de distemper, twel, bimeby, I begin fer ter feel de trestle-wuk give way, an' den I des know'd dat I wuz gwineter gitter racket. I slipt inter bed one Chuseday night, an' I never slip out no mo' fer mighty nigh er mont'.

"Nex' mornin' de meezles 'd done kivered me, an' den ef I didn't git dosted by de ole 'oman I'm a Chinee. She gimme back rashuns er sassafac tea. I des natally hankered an' got hongry atter water, an' ev'y time I sing out fer water I got b'ilin' hot sassafac tea. Hit got so dat w'en I wake up in de mornin' de ole 'oman 'd des come 'long wid a kittle er tea an' fill

me up. Dey tells me 'roun' town dat chilluns don't git hurted wid de meezles, w'ich ef dey don't I wanter be a baby de nex' time dey hits dis place. All dis yer meezles bizness is bran'-new ter me. In ole times, 'fo' de wah, I ain't heer tell er no seventy-fi'-year-ole nigger grapplin' wid no meezles. Dey ain't ketchin' no mo'. is dey, boss?"

"Oh, no—I suppose not."

" 'Kase ef dey is, youk'n des put my name down wid de migrashun niggers."

XI

THE EMIGRANTS

WHEN Uncle Remus went down to the passenger depot one morning recently, the first sight that caught his eye was an old negro man, a woman, and two children sitting in the shade near the door of the baggage-room. One of the children was very young, and the quartet was altogether ragged and forlorn-looking. The sympathies of Uncle Remus were immediately aroused. He approached the group by forced marches, and finally unburdened his curiosity.

"Whar is you m'anderin' unter, pard?"

The old negro, who seemed to be rather suspicious, looked at Uncle Remus coolly, and appeared to be considering whether he should make any reply. Finally, however, he stretched himself and said:

"We er gwine down in de naberhoods er Tallypoosy, an' we ain't makin' no fuss 'bout it, nudder."

"I disremember," said Uncle Remus, thoughtfully, "whar Tallypoosy is."

"Oh, hit's out yan," replied the old man, motioning his head as if it was just beyond the iron gates of the depot. "Hit's down in Alabam. When we git dar, maybe we'll go on twel we gits ter Massasip."

"Is you got enny folks out dar?" inquired Uncle Remus.

"None dat I knows un."

"An' youer takin' dis 'oman an' deze chillun out dar whar dey dunno nobody? Whar's yo' perwisions?" eying a chest with a rope around it.

"Dem's our bed-cloze," the old negro explained, noticing the glance of Uncle Remus. "All de vittles what we got we e't 'fo' we started."

"An' you speck ter retch dar safe an' soun'? Whar's yo' ticket?"

"Ain"t got none. De man say ez how dey'd pass us thoo. I gin a man a fi'-dollar bill 'fo' I lef' Jonesboro, an' he sed dat settled it."

"Lemme tell you dis," said Uncle Remus, straightening up indignantly: "you go an' rob somebody an' git on de chain-gang, an' let de 'oman scratch 'roun' yer an' make 'er livin'; but don't you git on dem kyars

—don't you do it. Yo' bes' holt is de chain-gang. You
kin make yo' livin' dar w'en you can't make it nowhars else. But don't you git on dem kyars. Ef you
do, youer gone nigger. Ef you ain't got no money fer
ter walk back wid, you better des b'il' yo' nes' right
here. I'm a-talkin' wid de bark on. I done seed deze
yer Arkinsaw emmygrants come lopein' back, an'
some un 'em didn't have rags nuff on 'em fer ter hide
dere nakidness. You leave dat box right whar she is,
an' let de 'oman take wun young un an' you take de
udder wun, an' den you git in de middle er de big
road an' pull out fer de place whar you come fum.
I'm preachin' now."

Those who watched say the quartet didn't take the
cars.

XII

AS A MURDERER

UNCLE REMUS met a police officer recently.

"You ain't hear talk er no dead nigger nowhar dis
mawnin', is you, boss?" asked the old man earnestly.

"No," replied the policeman, reflectively. "No, I
believe not. Have you heard of any?"

" 'Pears unter me dat I come mighty nigh gittin'
some news 'bout dat size, an' dat's w'at I'm a huntin'
fer. Bekaze ef dey er foun' a stray nigger layin' 'roun'
loose, wid 'is bref gone, den I wanter go home an' git
my brekfus' an' put on some clean cloze, an' 'liver

myse'f up ter wunner deze yer jestesses er de peace, an' git a fa'r trial."

"Why, have you killed anybody?"

"Dat's w'at's I'm a 'quirin' inter now, but I wouldn't be sustonished ef I ain't laid a nigger out some'rs on de subbubs. Hit's done got so it's agin de law fer ter bus' loose an' kill a nigger, ain't it, boss?"

"Well, I should say so. You don't mean to tell me that you have killed a colored man, do you?"

"I speck I is, boss. I speck I done gone an' done it dis time, sho.' Hit's bin sorter growin' on me, an' it come ter a head dis mawnin', les my name ain't Remus, an' dat's w'at dey bin er callin' me sence I wuz ole er 'nuff fer ter scratch myse'f wid my lef' han'."

"Well, if you've killed a man, you'll have some fun, sure enough. How was it?"

"Hit wuz dis way, boss: I wuz layin' in my bed dis mawnin' sorter ruminatin' 'roun', when de fus news I know'd I year a fus' 'mong de chickens, an' den my brissels riz. I done had lots er trubble wid dem chickens, an' w'en I years wun un um squall my ve'y shoes comes ontied. So I des sorter riz up an' retch fer my ole muskit, and den I crope out er de back do', an' w'atter you reckin I seed?"

"I couldn't say."

"I seed de biggest, blackest nigger dat you ever laid eyes on. He shined like de paint on 'im was fresh. He hed done grabbed fo'er my forwardes' pullets. I crope up nigh do do', an' hollered an' axed 'im how he wuz a gittin' on, an' den he broke, an' ez he broke I jammed de gun in de small er his back and banged

aloose. He let a yell like forty yaller cats a courtin', an' den he broke. You ain't seed no nigger hump hisse'f like dat nigger. He tore down de well shelter and fo' pannils er fence, an' de groun' look like wunner deze yer harrycanes had lit dar and fanned up de yeath."

"Why, I thought you killed him?"

"He bleedzed ter be dead, boss. Ain't I put de

gun right on 'im? Seem like I feel 'im give way w'en she went off."

"Was the gun loaded?"

"Dat's w'at my ole 'oman say. She had de powder in dar, sho', but I disremember wedder I put de buckshot in, er wedder I lef' um out. Leas'ways, I'm gwineter call on wunner deze yer jestesses. So long, boss."

XIII

HIS PRACTICAL VIEW OF THINGS

"BRER REMUS, is you heern tell er deze doin's out yer in de udder eend er town?" asked a colored deacon of the church the other day.

"W'at doin's is dat, Brer Ab?"

"Deze yer signs an' wunders whar dat cullud lady died day 'fo' yistiddy. Mighty quare goin's on out dar, Brer Remus, sho's you bawn."

"Sperrits?" inquired Uncle Remus, sententiously.

"Wuss'n dat, Brer Remus. Some say dat jedgment-day ain't fur off, an' de folks is flockin' 'roun' de house a hollerin' an' a shoutin' des like dey wuz in er revival. In de winder glass dar you kin see de flags a flyin', an' Jacob's lather is dar, an' dar's writin' on de pane w'at no man can't read—leas'wise dey ain't none read it yit."

"W'at kinder racket is dis youer givin' un me now, Brer Ab?"

"I done bin dar, Brer Remus; I done seed um wid bofe my eyes. Cullud lady what wuz intranced done woke up an' say dey ain't much time fer ter tarry.

She say she meet er angel in de road, an' he p'inted straight fer de mornin' star, an' tell her fer ter prepar'. Hit look mighty cu'us, Brer Remus."

"Cum down ter dat, Brer Ab," said Uncle Remus, wiping his spectacles carefully, and readjusting them —"cum down ter dat, an' dey ain't nuthin' dat ain't cu'us. I ain't no spishus nigger myse'f, but I 'spizes fer ter year dogs a howlin' an' squinch-owls havin' de ager out in de woods, an' w'en a bull goes a bellerin' by de house den my bones git cole an' my flesh commences fer ter creep; but w'en it comes ter deze yer sines in de a'r an' deze yer sperrits in de woods, den I'm out—den I'm done. I is, fer a fack. I bin livin' yer

more'n seventy year, an' I year talk er niggers seein'
ghos'es all times er night an' all times er day, but I
ain't never seed none yit; an' deze yer flags an' Jacob's
lathers, I ain't seed dem, nudder."

"Dey er dar, Brer Remus."

"Hit's des like I tell you, Brer Ab. I ain't 'sputin'
'bout it, but I ain't seed um, an' I don't take no
chances deze days on dat w'at I don't see, an' dat
w'at I sees I got ter 'zamine mighty close. Lemme
tell you dis, Brer Ab: don't you let deze sines onsettle
you. W'en old man Gabrile toot his ho'n, he ain't
gwinter hang no sine out in de winder-panes, an'
when ole Fadder Jacob lets down dat lather er his'n
you'll be mighty ap' fer ter hear de racket. An' don't
you bodder wid jedgment-day. Jedgment-day is
lierbul fer ter take keer un itse'f."

"Dat's so, Brer Remus."

"Hit's bleedzed ter be so, Brer Ab. Hit don't
bodder me. Hit's done got so now dat w'en I gotter
pone er bread, an' a rasher er bacon, an' nuff grease
fer ter make gravy, I ain't keerin' much w'edder fokes
sees ghos'es er no."

XIV

THAT DECEITFUL JUG

UNCLE REMUS was in good humor one evening
recently when he dropped casually into the editorial

room of "The Constitution," as has been his custom
for the past year or two. He had a bag slung across
his shoulder, and in the bag was a jug. The presence
of this humble but useful vessel in Uncle Remus's bag
was made the occasion for several suggestive jokes at
his expense by the members of the staff, but the old
man's good humor was proof against all insinuations.

"Dat ar jug's bin ter wah, mon. Hit's wunner deze
yer ole timers. I got dat jug down dar in Putmon
County w'en Mars 'Lisha Perryman wuz a young
man, an' now he's done growed up, an' got ole an'
died, an' his chilluns is growed up an' dey kin count
dere gran'chilluns, an' yit dar's dat jug des ez lively
an' ez lierbul fer ter kick up devilment ez w'at she
wuz w'en she come fum de foundry."

"That's the trouble," said one of the young men.
"That's the reason we'd like to know what's in it
now."

"Now youer gittin' on ma'shy groun'," replied
Uncle Remus. "Dat's de p'int. Dat's w'at make me
say w'at I duz. I bin knowin' dat jug now gwine on
sixty-fi' year, an' de jug w'at's more seetful dan dat
jug ain't on de topside er de worrul. Dar she sets,"
continued the old man, gazing at it reflectively, "dar
she sets dez ez natchul ez er ambertype, an' yit
whar's de man w'at kin tell w'at kinder confab she's a
gwineter carry on w'en dat corn-cob is snatched
outen 'er mouf? Dat jug is mighty seetful, mon."

"Well, it don't deceive any of us up here," remarked the agricultural editor, dryly. "We've seen jugs before."

"I boun' you is, boss; I boun' you is. But you ain't seed no seetful jug like dat. Dar she sets a bellyin' out an' lookin' mighty fat an' full, an' yit she'd set dar a bellyin' out ef dere wuzent nuthin' but win' under dat stopper. You knows dat she ain't got no aigs in her, ner no bacon, ner no grits, ner no termar-tusses, ner no shellotes, an' dat's 'bout all you duz know. Dog my cats ef de seetfulness er dat jug don't git away wid me," continued Uncle Remus, with a chuckle. "I wuz comin' 'cross de bridge des now, an' Brer John Henry seed me wid de bag slung onter my back, an' de jug in it, an' he ups an' sez, sezee:

" 'Heyo, Brer Remus, ain't it gittin' late for water-millions?'

"Hit wuz de seetfulness er dat jug. If Brer John Henry know'd de color er dat watermillion, I speck he'd snatch me up 'fo' de confunce. I 'clar' ter grashus ef dat jug ain't a caution!"

"I suppose it's full of molasses now," remarked one of the young men, sarcastically.

"Hear dat!" exclaimed Uncle Remus, triumphantly —"hear dat! W'at I tell you? I sed dat jug wuz seetful, an' I sticks to it. I bin knowin' dat—"

"What has it got in it?" broke in some one; "molasses, kerosene, or train-oil?"

"Well, I lay she's loaded, boss. I ain't shuk her up sence I drapt in, but I lay she's loaded."

"Yes," said the agricultural editor, "and it's the meanest bug-juice in town—regular sorghum skimmings."

"Dat's needer yer ner dar," responded Uncle Remus. "Po' fokes better be fixin' up for Chrismus now w'ile rashuns is cheap. Dat's me. W'en I year Miss Sally gwine 'bout de house w'isslin' 'W'en I k'n Read my Titles Cler'—an' w'en I see de martins swawmin' atter sundown—an' w'en I year de peckerwoods confabbin' togedder dese moonshiny nights in my een' er town—den I knows de hot wedder's a breakin' up, an' I know it's 'bout time fer po' fokes fer ter be rastlin' 'roun' and huntin' up dere rashuns. Dat's me, up an' down."

"Well, we are satisfied. Better go and hire a hall," remarked the sporting editor, with a yawn. "If you are engaged in a talking match you have won the money. Blanket him somebody, and take him to the stable."

"An' w'at's mo'," continued the old man, scorning to notice the insinuation, "dough I year Miss Sally w'isslin', an' de peckerwoods a chatterin', I ain't seein' none er deze yer loafin' niggers fixin' up fer ter 'migrate. Dey kin holler Kansas all 'roun' de naberhood, but ceppin' a man come 'long an' spell it wid greenbacks, he don't ketch none er deze yer town niggers. You year me, dey ain't gwine."

"Stand him up on the table," said the sporting editor; "give him room."

"Better go down yer ter de calaboose, an' git some news fer ter print," said Uncle Remus, with a touch

of irony in his tone. "Some new nigger mighter broke inter jail."

"You say the darkeys are not going to emigrate this year?" inquired the agricultural editor, who is interested in these things.

"Shoo! dat dey ain't! I done seed an' I knows."

"Well, how do you know?"

"How you tell w'en crow gwineter light? Niggers bin prom'nadin' by my house all dis summer, holdin' dere heads high up an' de w'ites er dere eyeballs shinin' in de sun. Dey wuz too bigitty fer ter look over de gyardin' palin's. 'Long 'bout den de wedder wuz fetchin' de nat'al sperrits er turkentime outen de pine-trees an' de groun' wuz fa'rly smokin' wid de hotness. Now that it's gittin' sorter airish in de mornin's, dey don't 'pear like de same niggers. Dey done got so dey'll look over in de yard, an' nex' news you know de'll be tryin' fer ter scrape up 'quaintence wid de dog. W'en dey passes now dey looks at de chicken-coop an' at der tater-patch. W'en you see niggers gittin' dat familious, you kin 'pen' on dere campin' wid you de ballunce er de season. Day 'fo' yistiddy I kotch one un um lookin' over de fence at my shoats, an' I sez, sez I:

"'Duz you wanter purchis dem hogs?'

"'Oh, no,' sezee, 'I wuz des lookin' at dere p'ints.'

"'Well, dey ain't p'intin' yo' way,' sez I, 'an', fuddermo', ef you don't bodder 'longer dem hogs dey ain't gwineter clime outer dat pen an' 'tack you, nudder,' sez I.

"An' I boun'," continued Uncle Remus, driving the corn-cob stopper a little tighter in his deceitful jug and gathering up his bag—"an' I boun' dat my ole muskit'll go off 'tween me an' dat same nigger yit, an' he'll be at de bad een', an' dis seetful jug'll 'fuse ter go ter de funer'l."

XV

THE FLORIDA WATERMELON

"Look yer, boy," said Uncle Remus yesterday, stopping near the railroad crossing on Whitehall Street, and gazing ferociously at a small colored youth; "look yer, boy, I'll lay you out flat ef you come flingin' yo' watermillion rimes under my foot—you watch ef I don't. You k'n play yo' pranks on deze yer w'ite fokes, but w'en you come a cuttin' up yo' capers roun' me you'll lan' right in de middle uv er spell er sickness—now you mine w'at I tell you. An' I ain't gwine fer ter put up wid none er yo' sassness nudder —let 'lone flingin' watermillion rimes whar I kin git mixt up wid um. I done had nuff watermillions yistiddy an' de day befo'.'"

"How was that, Uncle Remus?" asked a gentleman standing near.

"Hit wuz sorter like dis, boss. Las' Chuseday, Mars John he fotch home two er deze yer Flurridy watermillions, an him an' Miss Sally sot down fer ter eat um. Mars John an' Miss Sally ain't got nuthin' dat's too good fer me, an' de fus news I know'd Miss Sally wuz a hollerin' fer Remus. I done smelt de watermillion on de a'r, an' I ain't got no better sense dan fer ter go w'en I years w'ite fokes a hollerin'—I larnt

daт w'en I wa'n't so high. Leas'ways I galloped up
ter de back po'ch, an' dar sot de watermillions dez
ez natchul ez ef dey'd er bin raised on de ole Spivey
place in Putmon County. Den Miss Sally, she cut me
off er slishe—wunner deze yer ongodly slishes, big ez
yo' hat, an' I sot down on de steps an' wrop myse'f
roun' de whole blessid chunk, 'cepin' de rime" Uncle
Remus paused and laid his hand upon his stomach as
if feeling for something.

"Well, old man, what then?"

"Dat's w'at I'm a gittin' at, boss," said Uncle Remus, smiling a feeble smile. "I santered roun' 'bout
er half nour, an' den I begin fer ter feel sorter

squeemish—sorter like I done bin an' swoller'd 'bout
fo' poun's off'n de ruff een' uv er scantlin'. Look like
ter me dat I wuz gwineter be sick, an' den hit look
like I wuzent. Bimeby a little pain showed 'is head
an' sorter m'andered roun' like he wuz a lookin' fer
a good place fer ter ketch holt, an' den a great big
pain jump up an' take atter de little one an' chase
'im 'roun' an' 'roun,' an' he mus' er kotch 'im, kaze
bimeby de big pain retch down an' grab dis yer lef'
leg—so—an' haul 'im up, an' den he retch down an'
grab de udder one an' pull him up, an' den de wah
begun, sho nuff. Fer mighty nigh fo' hours dey kep'
up dat racket, an' des ez soon ez a little pain 'ud
jump up de big un 'ud light onter it an' gobble it up,
an' den de big un 'ud go sailin' roun' huntin' fer mo'.
Some fokes is mighty cu'us, dough. Nex' mornin' I
hear Miss Sally a laughin', an' singin' an' a w'isslin'
des like dey want no watermillions raise in Flurridy.
But somebody better pen dis yer nigger boy up w'en
I'm on de town—I kin tell you dat."

XVI

UNCLE REMUS PREACHES TO A CONVERT

"Dey tells me you done jine de chu'ch," said Uncle
Remus to Pegleg Charley.

"Yes, sir," responded Charley, gravely, "dat's so."

"Well, I'm mighty glad er dat," remarked Uncle

Remus, with unction. "It's 'bout time dat I wuz spectin' fer ter hear un you in de chain-gang, an', stidder dat, hit's de chu'ch. Well, dey ain't no tellin' deze days whar a nigger's gwineter lan'."

"Yes," responded Charley, straightening himself up and speaking in a dignified tone, "yes, I'm fixin' to do better. I'm preparin' fer to shake worldliness. I'm done quit so'shatin' wid deze w'ite town boys.

Dey've been a goin' back on me too rapidly here lately, an' now I'm a goin' back on dem."

"Well, ef you done had de speunce un it, I'm mighty glad. Ef you got 'lijjun, you better hole on to it 'twell de las' day in de mornin'. Hit's mighty good fer ter kyar' 'roun' wid you in de day time an' likewise in de night time. Hit'll pay you mo' dan politics, an' ef you stan's up like you oughter, hit'll las' longer dan a bone-fellum. But you wanter have one er deze yer ole-time grips, an' you des gotter shet yo' eyes an' swing on like wunner deze yer bull-tarrier dogs."

"Oh, I'm goin' to stick, Uncle Remus. You kin put your money on dat. Deze town boys can't play no more uv dere games on me. I'm fixed. Can't you lend me a dime, Uncle Remus, to buy me a pie? I'm dat hongry dat my stomach is gittin' ready to go in mo'nin'."

Uncle Remus eyed Charley curiously a moment, while the latter looked quietly at his timber toe. Finally, the old man sighed and spoke:

"How long is you bin in de chu'ch, son?"

"Mighty near a week," replied Charley.

"Well, lemme tell you dis, now, 'fo' you go enny fudder. You ain't bin in dar long nuff fer ter go 'roun' takin up conterbutions. Wait ontwell you gits sorter seasoned like, an' den I'll hunt 'roun' in my cloze an' see ef I can't run out a thrip er two fer you. But don't you levy taxes too early."

Charley laughed, and said he would let the old man off if he would treat to a watermelon.

XVII

AS TO EDUCATION

As Uncle Remus came up Whitehall Street recently, he met a little colored boy carrying a slate and a number of books. Some words passed between them, but their exact purport will probably never be known. They were unpleasant, for the attention of a wandering policeman was called to the matter by hearing the old man bawl out:

"Don't you come foolin' longer me, nigger. Youer flippin' yo' sass at de wrong color. You k'n go roun'

yer an' sass deze w'ite people, an' maybe dey'll stan' it, but w'en you come a slingin' yo' jaw at a man w'at wuz gray w'en de fahmin' days gin out, you better go an' git yo' hide greased."

"What's the matter, old man?" asked a sympathizing policeman.

"Nothin', boss, 'ceppin I ain't gwineter hav' no nigger chillun a hoopin' an' a hollerin' at me w'en I'm gwine 'long de streets."

"Oh, well, school-children—you know how they are."

"Dat's w'at make I say w'at I duz. Dey better be home pickin' up chips. W'at a nigger gwineter l'arn outen books? I kin take a bar'l stave an' fling mo' sense inter a nigger in one minnit dan all de school-houses betwixt dis en de State er Midgigin. Don't talk, honey! Wid one bar'l stave I kin fa'rly lif' de vail er ignunce."

"Then you don't believe in education?"

"Hit's de ruinashun er dis country. Look at my gal. De ole 'oman sont 'er ter school las' year, an' now we dassent hardly ax 'er fer ter kyar de washin' home.

She done got beyant 'er bizness. I ain't larnt nuthin'
in books, 'en yit I kin count all de money I gits. No
use talkin', boss. Put a spellin'-book in a nigger's
han's, en right den en dar' you loozes a plow-hand. I
done had de speunce un it."

XVIII

A TEMPERANCE REFORMER

"YER come Uncle Remus," said a well-dressed
negro, who was standing on the sidewalk near James's
bank recently, talking to a crowd of barbers. "Yer
come Uncle Remus. I boun' he'll sign it."

"You'll fling yo' money away
ef you bet on it," responded
Uncle Remus. "I ain't turnin'
nothin' loose on chu'ch 'scrip-
tions. I wants money right now
fer ter git a pint er meal."

" 'Tain't dat."

"An' I ain't heppin fer ter
berry nobody. Much's I kin do
ter keep de bref in my own
body."

" 'Tain't dat, nudder."

"An' I ain't puttin' my han'
ter no reckommends. I'm fear'd

fer ter say a perlite wud 'bout myself, an' I des know
I ain't gwine 'roun' flatter'n up deze udder niggers."

"An' 'tain't dat," responded the darkey, who held
a paper in his hand. "We er gittin' up a Good Tempeler's lodge, an' we like ter git yo' name."

"Eh-eh, honey! I done see too much er dis nigger
tempunce. Dey stan' up mighty squar' ontwell dere
dues commence ter cramp um, an' dey don't stan' de
racket wuf a durn. No longer'n yistiddy I seed one er
de head men er one er dese Tempeler's s'cieties totin'
water fer a bar-room. He had de water in a bucket,
but dey ain't no tellin' how much red licker he wuz a
totin'. G'long, chile—jine yo' s'ciety an' be good ter
yo'se'f. I'm a gittin' too ole. Gimme th'ee er fo' drams
endurin' er de day, an' I'm mighty nigh ez good a
tempunce man ez de next un. I got ter scuffle fer
sump'n t'eat."

XIX

AS A WEATHER PROPHET

UNCLE REMUS was enlightening a crowd of negroes
at the car-shed yesterday.

"Dar ain't nuthin'," said the old man, shaking his
head pensively, "dat ain't got no change wrote on it.
Dar ain't nothin dat ain't spotted befo' hit begins fer
ter commence. We all speunces dat p'overdence w'at

lifts us up fum one place an' sets us down in de udder. Hit's continerly a movin' an' a movin'.'"

"Dat's so!" "Youer talkin' now!" came from several of his hearers.

"I year Miss Sally readin' dis mawnin," continued the old man, "dat a man wuz comin' down yer fer ter take keer er de wedder—wunner deze yer Buro mens w'at goes 'roun' a puttin' up an' pullin' down."

"W'at he gwine do 'roun' yer?" asked one.

"He's a gwineter rege- late de wedder," replied Uncle Remus, senten- tiously. "He's a gwineter fix hit up so dat dere won't be so much worri- ment 'mong de w'ite fokes 'bout de kinder wedder w'at falls to dere lot."

"He gwine dish em up," suggested one of the older ones "like man dish out sugar."

"No," answered Uncle Remus, mopping his benign features with a very large and very red bandana. "He's a gwineter fix um better'n dat. He's a gwineter fix um up so you kin have any kinder wedder w'at you want widout totin' her home."

"How's dat?" asked some one.

"Hit's dis way," said the old man, thoughtfully. "In co'se you knows w'at kinder wedder you wants. Well, den, w'en de man comes 'long, w'ich Miss Sally say he will, you des gotter go up dar, pick out yo' wedder an' dere'll be a clock sot fer ter suit yo' case, an' w'en you git home, dere'll be yo' wedder a settin' out in de yard waitin' fer you. I wish he wuz yer now," the old man continued. "I'd take a p'ar er frosts in mine, ef I kotched cold fer it. Dat's me!"

There were various exclamations of assent, and the old man went on his way singing, "Don't you Grieve Atter Me."

XX

THE OLD MAN'S TROUBLES

"What makes you look so lonesome, Brer Remus?" asked a well-dressed negro, as the old man came shuffling down the street by James's corner yesterday.

"Youer mighty right, I'm lonesome, Brer John Henry. W'en a ole nigger like me is gotter paddle de canoe an' do de fishin' at de same time, an' w'en you bleedzd ter ketch de fish an' dassent turn de paddle loose fer ter bait de hook, den I tell you, Brer John, youer right whar de mink had de goslin'. Mars John and Miss Sally, dey done bin gone down unto Putmon County fer ter see der kinfolks mighty nigh

fo' days, an' you better b'leeve I done bin had ter
scratch 'roun' mighty lively fer ter make de rashuns
run out even."

"I wuz at yo' house las' night, Brer Remus," remarked Brer John Henry, "but I couldn't roust you
outer bed."

"Hit was de unseasonableness er de hour, I speck,"
said Uncle Remus, dryly.
" 'Pears unto me dat you all
chu'ch deacons settin' up
mighty late deze cole nights.
You'll be slippin' round arter
hours some time er nudder,
an' you'll slip bodaciously inter de calaboose. You mine
w'at I tell you.

"It's mighty cole wedder,"
said Brer John Henry, evidently wishing to change the
subject.

"Cole!" exclaimed Uncle Remus; "hit got pas' cole
on der quarter stretch. You oughter come to my house
night 'fo' las'. Den you'd a foun' me 'live an' kickin'.'"

"How's dat?"

"Well, I tell you, Brer John Henry, de cole wuz so
cole, an' de kiver wuz so light, dat I thunk I'd make a
raid on Mars John's shingle pile, an' out I goes an'
totes in a whole armful. Den I gits under de kiver an'

tells my ole 'oman fer ter lay 'em onto me like she was roofin' a house. Bimeby she crawls in, an' de shingles w'at she put on her side fer ter kiver wid, dey all drap off on de flo'. Den up I gits an' piles 'em on agin, an' w'en I gits in bed my shingles draps off, an' dat's de way it wuz de whole blessid night. Fus' it wuz me up an' den de ole 'oman, an' it kep' us pow'ful warm, too, dat kinder exercise. Oh, you oughter drapt roun' 'bout dat time, Brer John Henry. You'd a year'd sho' nuff cussin'!"

"You don't tell me, Brer Remus!"

"My ole 'oman say de Ole Boy wouldn't a foun' a riper nigger, ef he wer' ter scour de country fum Ferginny ter de Alabam!"

XXI

THE FOURTH OF JULY

UNCLE REMUS made his appearance recently with his right arm in a sling and his head bandaged to that extent that it looked like the stick made to accompany the Centennial bass-drum. The old man evidently expected an attack all around, for he was unusually quiet, and fumbled in his pockets in an embarrassed manner. He was not mistaken. The agricultural editor was the first to open fire:

"Well, you old villain! what have you been up to now?"

"It is really singular," remarked a commencement orator, "that not even an ordinary holiday—a holiday, it seems to me, that ought to arouse all the latent instincts of patriotism in the bosom of American citizens—can occur without embroiling some of our most valuable citizens. It is really singular to me that such a day should be devoted by a certain class of our population to broils and fisticuffs."

This final moral sentiment, which was altogether an impromptu utterance, and which was delivered with the air of one who addresses a vast but invisible audience of young ladies in white dresses and blue sashes, seemed to add to the embarrassment of Uncle Remus, and at the same time to make an explanation necessary.

"Dey ain't none er you young w'ite men never had no 'casion fer ter strike up wid one er deze Mobile niggers?" asked Uncle Remus. "'Kaze ef you iz, den you knows wharbouts de devilment come in. Show me a Mobile nigger," continued the old man, "an' I'll show you a nigger dat's marked for de chaingang. Hit may be de fote er de fif' er July, er hit may be de twelf' er Jinawerry, but w'en a Mobile nigger gits in my naberhood right den an' dar trubble sails in an' 'gages bode fer de season. I speck I'm ez fon' er deze Nunited States ez de nex' man w'at knows dat de Buro is busted up; but long ez Remus kin stan' on his hine legs no Mobile nigger can't flip inter

dis town longer no Wes' P'int 'schushun an' boss
'roun' 'mong de cullud fokes. Dat's me, up an' down,
an' I boun' dere's a nigger some'rs on de road dis
blessid day dat's got dis put away in his 'membunce."

"How did he happen to get you down and maul
you in this startling manner?" asked the commencement orator, with a tone of exaggerated sympathy in
his voice.

"Maul who?" exclaimed Uncle Remus, indignantly. "Maul who? Boss, de nigger dat mauled me
ain't bornded yit, an' dey er got ter have anudder
war 'fo one is bornded."

"Well, what was the trouble?"

"Hit wuz sorter dis way, boss. I wuz stannin' down

dere by Mars John Jeems's bank, chattin' wid Sis
Tempy, w'ich I ain't seed 'er befo' now gwine on
seven year, an' watchin' de folks trompin' by, w'en
one er deze yer slick-lookin' niggers, wid a bee-gum
hat an' a brass watch ez big ez de head uv a beer-
bar'l, come 'long an' bresh up agin me—so. Dere
wuz two un um, an' dey went 'long gigglin' an'
laffin' like a nes'ful er yaller-hammers. Bimeby dey
come 'long agin an' de smart Ellick brush up by me
once mo'. Den I say to myse'f, 'I lay I fetch you ef
you gimme anudder invite.' An', sho' 'nuff, yer he
come agin, an' dis time he rub a piece er watermillion rime under my lef' year."

"What did you do?"

"Me? I'm a mighty long-sufferin' nigger, but he
hadn't no mo'n totch me 'fo' I flung dese yer bones in
his face." Here Uncle Remus held up his damaged
hand triumphantly. "I sorter sprained my han', boss,
but dog my cats if I don't b'leeve I spattered de nigger's eyeballs on de groun', and w'en he riz his count'-
nence look fresh like beef-haslett. I look mighty
spindlin' an' puny now, don't I, boss?" inquired the
old man, with great apparent earnestness.

"Rather."

"Well, you des oughter see me git my Affikin up.
Dey useter call me er bad nigger long 'fo' de war, an'
hit looks like ter me dat I gits wuss an' wuss. Brer

John Henry say dat I oughter supdue my rashfulness, an' I don't 'spute it, but tu'n a Mobile nigger loose in dis town, fote er July or no fote er July, an', me er him, one is got ter lan' in jail. Hit's proned inter me."

THE END

761W

8191W